© 2018 Kendrai Meeks

Beauty & the Betrayer

Published by: Kendrai Meeks/Tulipe Noire Press

Text Design by: The Last TK

Edited by: Rebecca Hodgkins

Cover Design by: Mario Lampic

ISBN-10:

ISBN-13:

KENDRAI MEEKS

# BEAUTY
## AND THE
# BETRAYER

### RED HOOD ORIGINS
#### BOOK ONE

Many of us live in dysfunctional families, and so even if it's in a fairy tale, or perhaps because it's in a fairy tale, we have a chance to look at that side of our reflected lives differently.

-Kenneth Branagh

# ONE

Even as Gerwalta trailed her eldest sister down from the keep, the silver in her had pooled and transformed, changing its contours with the whims of her mind. Though the outer bailey walls of Schloss Wolfsretter would bar a werewolf's entry, the sword she'd visualized into being would be a critical weapon if the beast came looking for a fight.

"West gate, and hurry," Helga directed.

Gerwalta doubled her pace. Even lacking time in the field to intimately predict lupine nature, she deduced that a single wolf, alone and wearing his laymen form, willingly approaching the sacred fortress of the House of Red, wasn't looking for a fight. Unless he *wanted* to die, in which case his wish would be granted forthwith.

"A short sword?" Helga looked back over her youngest sibling's shoulder to inspect the armament she'd shaped. "Explain your rationale."

Why did all her sisters treat her as if she were still in the midst of her training? Even her sole brother, Maximilian, criticized her, despite her natural superiority as a woman. Gerwalta had claimed her fire six months ago, under the light of the Snow Moon. She was a righteous hood now, blessed with the ability to wield silver and a recognized wolfsretter of the clan. Even if Helga was ten years her senior and the heir apparent to their mother, *she* was not Matron yet.

Tradition demanded Gerwalta show respect to her elders, even if said elders annoyed her with the constant reminder that she was the baby of the family.

"He comes alone, in the form of a man. He does not bellow and he does not brood." Gerwalta had seen as much from the tower where she'd been tasked as the lookout when first he'd approached. "He exhibits no signs of open hostility. His gate is steady, his mannerisms gentle. Tentative, even. He will speak gently, drawing us near. If a weapon is called for, the conflict will be in close proximity. The short sword will allow me lethal force with maximum maneuverability."

"Might you not raise tensions by bearing a weapon upon his arrival?"

Gerwalta pulled ahead of her sister, keeping the sword at her side. "Speak not to me of tensions when a werewolf is at our hearth."

The Schloss Wolfretter was a proper castle, if a small one, it did not have the moat her cousin's in the Rhineland did. Given that the west wall sat precariously perched on the edge of a cliff high above the forest valley, how could it?

The wolf must have sensed their approach as much as they recognized his presence halfway across the outer bailey, but he did not turn. *What curious behavior*, Gerwalta thought, *to keep an eye to the woods and not to the enemy at your back.*

"Wolf!" Helga pushed her little sister aside, forcing Gerwalta to flank her. "Speak and declare by what gull or gullibility have you come here uninvited."

"I wish to present a petition to the Matron."

Gerwalta clicked her tongue. "Only the konigswolf may petition my mother."

His body shook with silent laughter as he pivoted. "Is that so?"

When his amused gaze met hers, Gerwalta realized that the supplicant did not need his fur to be a threat. Most wolves had dark features, but this one bucked that expectation. Blazing green eyes, and hair neither blonde nor brown, but a smattering of both. God had taken great effort in molding the clay of his anatomy. Tone, lithe, long-limbed. He used his lupine eyes as weapons, letting them fall upon her figure. And what sharp blades they were; his stare pierced Gerwalta deep within, making her weapon hand slack. The sword sunk to her side, as did her hostilities.

She'd been told some wolves could be devilishly handsome, but no one had said as handsome as the devil himself. His crooked grin melted her metal. *An animal nature, raw and unrefined, that speaks to our own,* the Matron had said, adding, *but never forget,* they *are the animals, and we, the masters.*

She'd expected ragged clothing, for the wolves of their

territory were merely farmers and didn't claim the wealth the wolfsretter did. His clothes, however, were quite fine. Not made from exotic fabrics as her formal attire was, but still, dignified.

And they fit him nicely. *Ever* so nicely.

"He *is* the konigswolf." Helga turned biting words on her younger sibling, forcing Gerwalta back to the moment.

"Though only recently so. You can be forgiven for not knowing, Fraulein." The king of the pack paid no mind to Helga, keeping his gaze fixed on Gerwalta. "You must be Fourth Daughter, the one who does not come to the packlands."

Helga ignored *him* in turn, also talking to Gerwalta. "Notify the castellan to raise the gate and send word to the Matron that an official audience has been requested. And, for the sake of St. Peter, stop staring at him, silly girl!"

"There's no call to demean the child, Frau Helga," the wolf said, leaning into the iron bars of the castle gate. "Let her look all she likes. It's only by accepting our ignorance that we can correct it, and the Matron has chosen to let this child remain quite ignorant."

Gerwalta sneered. All he had to do was open that pretty mouth to reveal his ugly inner nature. "Keep your silence, wolf, unless I should be forced to make you whimper."

The wolf's grin widened, setting Gerwalta's blood boiling. Ah, yes, there it was. Vanity, assumption, familiarity: all vices that wolves held in spades. Oh, he was dangerous, but he didn't need claws or teeth to be so. All he needed was that intoxicating, seductive smile.

Silver was in no short supply here, nor was its acquisition difficult. While owning the mines had made the wolfsretter wealthy, it had not, as with others who dug at the veins, deformed them. The righteous needed no pick or ax to pull the ore from the earthen holds below ground. All she needed was her power, her awoken supernatural ability to wield the precious metal and command its obeisance. In Gerwalta's hand, a chunk of silver could become an arrowhead, a dagger, a needle, a shield.

In this moment, as Helga's power fell over the metal grated to her hands in the form of gauntlets, it could be used to form manacles.

She held them up at eye level. "You know our procedure."

II

The wolf, taken aback but also visibly stealing himself, nodded. "I do."

"And you agree?"

"Mark my words, Frau Helga, I would not readily suffer such torture without need." The wolf presented his hands, fingers caked in dirt. "I submit to your hold."

The manacles again became liquid, pooling on Helga's open palm. As she pushed her hands through the grating of the iron gate, the metal began to siphon off, wrapping itself around the wolf's wrist. Searing flesh bubbled and baked. To his credit, the konigswolf merely winced, although the pain must have overwhelmed him. Even now, Gerwalta could see the tortured flesh under the metal weeping blood. Gerwalta back walked from her vantage point, wondering what in Christ's Kingdom could provoke one of his kind to endure so excruciating torment. She, for one, would never be able to stomach it.

And certainly, never for the "privilege" of being in the Matron's presence.

# TWO

Schloss Wolfsretter had never fallen to a foe's attack. It was guarded from the world of man by a tightly-woven forest lattice the laity called the *Schwarzwald*. Inside the Black Forest, the House of Red had built their fortress at the edge of a cliff, high above the valley floor. Only the west and south gates permitted entry, even the paths leading to those so narrow and treacherous, it was customary to tie blinders to the horses pulling the carts that would occasionally traverse the road, lest they panic and fall off the trail as it clung to the edge of the mountain.

In ancient times, a massive tree had grown on the cliff. It was said that, under its branches the first red Matron, Hlin the Conqueror, slew the Konigswolf Kroon, establishing the clan's dominion. The compound had grown around the tree, and even now, hundreds of years later, the base remained, carved to seat Hlin's progeny. This throne, a twisting upheaval of wood and antler melded by metallic threads and embellishments, sat at the back of the third inner chamber. From it, Gunda Faust presided over both her family and the forest with a silver fist.

The Red Matron, they said, never smiled but in private moments of pleasure and in the execution of slaughter. No exception would be granted for the wolf who groveled before her now, pleased though she must be with such an act of obeisance. With a nod, First Daughter laid a hand on his human shoulder, forcing him to the ground.

"Andreas Baron."

Frau Gunda Faust pronounced his name like a slur, as she had the several times they'd encountered each other since Andreas had risen as king. He thought, it must please her that he should have to accost her here, in her own castle, surrounded by the trappings of her station, wearing the pelt of one of his ancestors.

"Speak."

At the Matron's command, Andreas touched his forehead with the fingers of his right hand before covering his chest and dotting the floor with his brow. He then lifted his head only enough to show his eyes.

His rough voice bore witness to the pain induced by his silver manacles. "I would make a petition, Matron, if you would hear it."

"*If* I would hear it?" she barked, bringing herself to the edge of her throne. "Are you suggesting that I would be reticent in my duties as Matron? Do you question my competence to rule your pack?"

His eyes cast downward as his palms flattened on the floor, leaving him fully prostrate. "I did not mean to imply such. As you know, I am only in the third moon of my kingship, and still unfamiliar with the ways of court. Please overlook any gaff of protocol."

"You are on your knees, and that is a start. Look up, Konigswolf." She waved a hand dismissively. "Proceed."

He did as commanded, bringing his bound hands up, steepling them into his chest. Blood from his veins burned by silver trickled down his forearms and soaked into his darkening sleeve. "I request permission to leave the Schwarzwald, to reclaim one of my pack who left last night."

That brought the Matron to the front of her throne. "A rogue or an exile?"

"I'm not certain, Matron." Andreas shifted, shying his eyes away. "As I said, I am still learning to properly wield my power as Konigswolf. In anger, I neglected to recall how my words can bind action. I cannot recall my exact wording, if I gave an order for my brother to leave, or merely suggested it. In any case, I could not intercede ere Stephen had departed. If I *did* command his departure, he'd be powerless to return unless I seek him out and remove the obligation of the edict. I must have my brother in my pack; you know his value to me."

"Your pack's situation is not without remedy. We have discussed this. Why not wait for him to return? Brothers quarrel, men take respites to let rows clear."

"Matron, I'm afraid it is more than that. You see, the reason we quarreled was that Stephen informed me that he wishes to wed a member of the laity. Ordinarily, I would entertain such considerations, but the object of his desire is a member of the imperial court in some way. Exposing a bride of status to our world comes with consequences.

I fear that he has set out in some rueful attempt to claim her, against my wishes." The wolf licked his lips before adding, "The moon grows fuller by the night."

The Matron's skin went white. "He would reveal our kind to the world, to man, church, and emperor."

"I know your veiled interactions with the court are of great import to your wealth and power. I say this not to judge. I merely wish to acknowledge that his retrieval is critical for both the prosperity of your clan and the sanctity of my pack."

"Not to mention for the continued secrecy of our kind." Andreas had never seen the Matron so red-faced. "So newly a king, and already, you have let lambs go astray. It puts your leadership in question, Herr Baron. Even that you allowed your own kin to become entwined with a laywoman…"

"That sin falls to my predecessor." Heat fringed the edges of his words as he dared cut off the Matron. Realizing his mistake, he resumed groveling. "Apologies, but we are of the same mind in this. I beg, permit me leave to pursue Stephen and retrieve him. I vow that I shall return with my scoundrel of a brother forthwith and that he shall be immediately mated on my orders to one who will anchor him to the pack."

The Matron fanned a silver coin through her fingers. Where had it come from? Her command, of course. Moments before, it had been a ring on her finger. "And if your brother proves to be beyond your reach?"

The wolf faltered, losing three shades of color. "I shall do what's needed."

"Really?" Amusement made the Matron's tone suddenly light. "You would kill your own brother? Even if you think you mean that, Herr Baron, I do not believe you capable, when nip comes to bite. Your words failed to deter him, why would your maw be any different?"

"If the good of my pack must come before the viability of my bloodline, then it must. Would you not do the same, Matron? To secure your clan, would you not shed your own blood?"

That comment brought the Matron to her feet, a sudden burst of movement that made the konigswolf flinch. But it was not to attack that she rose, but to draw attention to her family's presence.

"Helga." The Matron descended from her dais, brushing the cheek of each of her children in turn. "Gretchen. Zelda. Maximillian," and pulled back just enough to abstain from touching the youngest. "Gerwalta. My five children are like the fingers of the hand which clutches my sword. Should one become diseased—" She paused, lacing the fingers of her hand around the youngest offspring's throat, squeezing just enough to make Gerwalta flinch. "It would grieve me, but yes."

Andreas couldn't believe his eyes, or his ears. Nor, did it seem, could Fourth Daughter, whose anger flushed her cheeks ere she lashed her head aside. The konigswolf became heartsick when he thought it may be his fate to end his own brother, but his brother was responsible for his own downfall. But to end one's own child?

And *they* considered *him* the animal?

The moment passed, and the Matron turned again on the supplicant. "Is your second prepared to mind your pack until your return?"

"Yes, Matron. Angser is a capable wolf who believes in firm discipline. He can be counted on to keep peace until my return."

"He must, or I will dispatch him without consultation," the Matron assured. "You are right insofar as saying your brother's revelations would affect us both. Thus, I too have a vested interest in either his return, or his destruction. I will grant your request to seek him… under the condition that one of my clan accompany your journey."

Silver slicked over the weapon hand of many a wolfsretter as a growl curdled in the wolf's throat. His mouth bore witness to his condition, his teeth growing long and pointed.

"I do not require a minder. I am *konigswolf.*"

The Matron descended upon him with bladed fingertips crowned in silver. She pulled back a hand before letting it fly forward, the metal burning marks into the wolf's cheek. "This is my condition. Accept it, or I will send *two* of my clan in your stead, with orders to kill on sight. If you want a chance to save him, you will take what I offer."

To his credit, Andreas did not whimper. With eyes closed, he ate the pain. "Frau Helga and Frau Zelda know Stephen's face best."

"Helga is with child. She cannot leave the forest." The Matron turned back to the dais, where each of her brood remained in quiet obeisance. "Gerwalta will accompany you."

Andreas sneered. "She is but a child."

"She *is* young, but righteous nonetheless, and my own blood. Though she lacks experience of overseeing your pack, she is a capable warrior. Should retrieving your brother prove troublesome, she will dispatch him posthaste. Prepare yourself, then. You leave at sunrise."

# THREE

"This is preposterous."

Away from court, where cousins, visiting wolfsretter of other clans, the families of her siblings, and select trusted laity always lurked with open eyes and contagious tongues, Gerwalta could share with her mother her exact thoughts.

"What do we care if one wolf has gone chasing after a laymaiden?" the youngest Faust bemoaned. "When full moon comes, he will take his wolf, ravage whatever poor village or hamlet he finds himself in, and be killed for his misdeeds posthaste. The problem solves itself."

"And let innocent laity die?" Gunda dropped a few more pfennige into the purse at her daughter's waist before tucking the pouch of coins behind the dark green folds of skirting. She'd travel with silver, of course, but the lower denomination could be used to avoid attention. "The primary reason for our existence is to protect them from the wolves. I would have dispatched one of your sisters upon learning of Stephen Baron's intention for that reason alone, even if Andreas had not sought to retrieve him. And that is the primary mission you are to undertake: protect the laity."

"Primary?" Gerwalta repeated the word as though having just learned it. "What other task would merit this journey?"

"You heard the konigswolf. Stephen's beloved travels with the imperial court. Mayhap your travels will take you into the sphere of power, where I would have you... *listen*."

Gerwalta narrowed her eyes on her mother. "For what?"

"For some indication of why favor has turned from us."

Incredulity crept into Gerwalta's tone. "Who else besides us could supply the crown with silver at such low cost, or match our craftsmanship?"

Gunda sharpened her gaze, giving her youngest the kind of drawn-out silence that demanded her to reassess her conclusion. Gerwalta combed memory, myth, and the moment for evidence that could weigh against her supposition.

"Precisely the question to ask, daughter." The Matron let her chin dip once. "The Ottomans may have let Vienna slip through their fingers, but their campaign brought more than laymen soldiers to the empire's borders. When the Grand Turk withdrew, his remaining footprints filled with the consequences of his quest."

"But you couldn't possibly believe the Emperor's court would conduct business with the House of Black, or vampires, even." Her mother nodded. "But... they are Saracens! How could the *Holy Roman Emperor*, the great defender of the Church, favor Muslims over Catholic subjects?"

"Profits change men's allegiances faster than gods. But that is not what's bothering me. What I wish to know," Gunda paused, examining the silver bands that encircled her wrists, "is what the black hoods are trying to achieve by selling cheap silver to the crown. If they are merely raising funds to return home, let them make haste. If they are settling in with intents to settle west... Well, then, we'll need to plan accordingly. This is why I chose you to be my emissary on this mission. Even though your experience with lupines is limited, your training in laity court procedures and politics is more thorough than your sisters'. You are my progeny; you will always be a wolfsretter first, but what I need on this mission is a daughter who can spin intrigues as well as silver."

"Then, you would like me to let Stephen Baron make it as far as court?"

"Just be certain he is not there come full moon. As soon as he's made it far enough to provide an excuse for visiting the emperor's court, do away with the lone wolf. Keep up the illusion that you are merely an overseer, for the moment Andreas Baron understands we are using this crisis to our advantage, he will either turn on you, or turn away from you. Neither serves our purposes."

The young hood bowed, the grin carved by pride barely hidden. "Understood."

"Good. Keep your wits about you. Never let that wolf from your sight, and do not hesitate to strike him or his brother down should they pose a danger."

# FOUR

They left at dawn, at an hour in which both would rather have taken to their beds than dragged themselves away from home. Gerwalta hoped her brother was right. As a man, Maximillian was often called upon to conduct the family's business with the laity, a vulgar race who thought women the weaker sex. As such, Max often had to adapt the rhythm of his duties to day. "Sleeping at night, and waking *with* the sun instead of the moon..." he'd said to her as he helped Gerwalta pack her sack. "It feels wrong, but after a day or two, one learns to tolerate it."

Halfway through the sun's arc across the sky on this first day, doubts festered. Gerwalta prided herself on her dutifulness; she would *not* let the konigswolf from her sight. She *did* wish, however, that Herr Baron would slow down. As was custom among wolfsretter, Gerwalta tracked the wolf-like prey, but from the safety of the treetops. She nimbly leaped from oak to pine, trailing the wolf, but keeping him in sight. He drove forward with a veracity that had her weaving through branches like a needle through cloth to keep apace. His stamina... where did he get it? It might be easier to walk on the road beside him, but Gerwalta didn't feel it proper, acting as though the wolf were her equal.

Nonetheless, when Herr Baron paused to rest shortly past midday, she *almost* thanked him. Was he oblivious to her observation from the branches above, or indifferent to it? Her body tingled with the innate gift of her kind: the sense of knowing when a lupine was near. Did wolves have the same ability? How had it never occurred to her to ask that?

"You'll have a difficult time as we descend into the next valley."

His sudden words drew her from her reverie. By whatever means, he at least knew she was within earshot, it seemed.

She sat down on a branch. "I will endure."

"Not up there, scurrying like a squirrel in pursuit. The trees are younger farther on, unlikely to bear even your graceful form."

Her form's bearing on the trees was hardly the issue, but he need not know the particulars of why. Not even her own mother had been able to learn that piece of knowledge, and Gerwalta well intended that the Matron should never become aware of the secret her daughter hid.

Herr Baron settled onto a large boulder, making a show of unpacking his food stores. He ripped into a hunk of bread (she smelled cheese too, if she wasn't mistaken), his jaw working hard to consume what even now must be beginning to lose its freshness. "Do you think, Fraulein, that I am merely waiting until we are a goodly distance from Schloss Wolfsretter to turn and rip you, limb from limb? I assure you, I haven't the slightest intention. Not to mention, it is midday. I am never weaker in the passage of time. So why not come down, already?"

"Do you think that you can command my presence, and I'll obey?"

"I will never command anything of you. An honorable wolf does no such thing; he offers what he is happy to give. Even if you are a wolfsretter and in any other situation, I wouldn't be concerned at all with the way you go about doing things. Walk all the way to Ulster on your hands and wearing a bell, for all I care. But you were tasked with accompanying me, and I know you obey your Matron like my wolves obey my order."

"A poor comparison, given our quest."

The jibe dented his demeanor, and she observed with glee as Herr Baron grimaced. Nonetheless, he pressed on. "If I attempt to escape you, it will have ramifications for my pack. We are stuck together on this sojourn, no matter that either of us would under any other circumstances eat a salad of hemlock than spend time together. I must make haste to retrieve Stephen as quickly as possible, which means that *you also* must make haste to keep up with me. Since I'm obligated to stay on two feet, not four, the road delivers us to my brother fastest. Already I have slowed too much to allow you to keep apace, jumping from tree to tree, but no more. Please, come down, partake of your stocks, and rest. We'll be underway again soon enough. You have my word, I will make no attempt to harm you."

She dropped from the trees in a squat, her cloak pooling around her, a length of two klafters separating them. As a wolf, he could have crossed the distance in two bounds. As a man, he'd first have to struggle to his feet, giving her time to leap away should he try.

"A sword can always injure, even when it is rusty."

His amused smile annoyed her. "Is that what you think of me? Nothing more than a warmonger?"

"You are a wolf."

"I am a man."

"You are both," she snapped, rising to her feet. "And a man, while less deadly, may be of no better intent."

"Speak from experience?" He dusted the last crumbs of his meal from his lap. "You seem so young to have felt the pain of a man's deception."

"I have encountered as yet no man who would dare deceive me." Ire bite into Gerwalta's words, and she knew from countless lessons that one must keep emotions in check when dealing with a wolf. "I would not flaunt seniority over me when you have little ground to claim it."

"The number of moons between us may compare, but I am a konigswolf, and you, merely a fourth daughter."

As he stood, raising a hand, she took a step back. Only after a moment did she realize he held a skin of water. Hers had run out earlier in the morning, and so intent was she with keeping up with him, that she hadn't had opportunity to deviate from the road to replenish it as yet.

"Go on, drink," he encouraged, raising the skin higher. "You're far too loud when you move, and you lack grace in your leaps."

She made to spit back his venom in kind, but he cut her off.

"I do not criticize to spite you. I'm only pointing out that it's causing you to lose strength too fast. I can hear how breathless you've been, hopping from tree to tree in an effort to remain both hidden and in position. The tactic is a good policy when pursuing a wolf in a limited space. It does not adapt well to sustained, long road journeys. You've not imbibed in nearly an hour; you must be parched."

How infuriatingly presumptive he was. "As I said, I will endure."

"You will fall ill," Andreas retorted. "And if I miss an opportunity to save my brother because I had to stop and nurse you back to health, I would ally with your mother in her anger. Drink, and when we start off again, save your energy by walking with me. Your mother bade mind me, but she did not say it had to be done covertly. That is an improvisation of your own design."

The speed with which she snatched the skin from his hand must have shocked him. Herr Baron's eyes widened with wonderment as she tipped the vessel and poured the water down her throat. Gerwalta had only begun to ease her posture when he spoke again.

"Remove your cloak."

Gerwalta lowered the water skin to find his hungry eyes focused on her throat where a rivulet of water, having overflowed her mouth, trickled into the fabric of her dressings. "How *dare* you?"

"By my fang, are all wolfsretter as vain as you?" The wolf shut his eyes, exhaling. "The common laity do not wear such brightly-colored cloth. You will give yourself away as a wealthy woman and they will conspire to rob you."

"I am a wealthy woman, and you speak as though any layman could get the better of me."

"I am quite certain they could not. But here, young ladies—at least those of proper learning and some social standing— do not conjure silver spears and impale those attempting to take advantage of them." Andreas pulled the skin from her hands and tucked it back into his satchel. "Remove the cloak, for my sake, if not yours. We can hide it in your sack, or if that proves insufficient we… can… Oh, my."

The wolf's words died in his throat as Gerwalta's red cloak turned to dust and flitted to the ground. Even a mythic beast as he was, as *they both were*, he marveled.

"You simply made it disappear."

Gerwalta inspected herself for defect before cawing a laugh. "Do not tell me you were unaware of our ability?"

"Should I have been, would I be in such awe?" He ventured closer, hunting for evidence of what had been there moments before and trying not to make her flinch. No good; three steps had her pulling back. "Can all wolfsretter do this?"

"Only the righteous. And I do not know why it should surprise you. Do not you conceal fang and fur in the light of day?"

"As is evident, Fraulein." Andreas held out his arms wide, calling far too much attention to a body she shouldn't appreciate so much. "Can you make all your clothing disappear?"

He barely managed to step back in time to avoid her smack, holding out his hands in supplication. "That came out wrong. My apologies. Only... witnessing such craft does birth a number of questions to a curious mind."

She paused a moment, as though weighing her next words. She knew the fundamentals of her kind's practices, and by consequence, many facts about lupines. Still, as the youngest child of a fearsome Matron, her curiosity had never been encouraged. Perhaps Herr Baron would prove a more willing tutor than her older siblings.

"I, too... have questions."

His frame eased. "I would attempt to answer them, if I can."

She couldn't stop her grin. "First, why have you not taken your wolf for this journey?"

"Do you not recall? The matron bade me travel as would a layman."

"She said *sleep* in times as would they. *That* interpretation is an improvisation on *your* part."

She didn't like to admit that a thrill ran through her when, turning his own words back on him, the wolf grinned.

"Surely you would travel much faster with four legs in place of two," Gerwalta continued.

"Do you not recall the farms we passed in the last valley?" He pointed back up the road they'd traveled. "No doubt word has reached you, as it has my pack, of the recent attacks on livestock in this valley? Natural wolves, of course; all my pack except my brother are accounted for, and he could not have done so much damage and in so little time. No, Fraulein. A farmer out this way would see a wolf in the light of day as no welcome thing, and as full moon approaches, I do not know that I would resist."

"But, *you* are a farmer."

A line creased between his eyes. "Indeed, and what of it?"

"Well, I mean... How is it that you do not slaughter your own stock when in the throes of your animal nature? And how do the animals you keep not bolt from your presence? I can smell your wolf nature even now. Surely, the pigs can too."

"I'm certain they do." A smile grew across his face as he placed a blade of grass nipped from the ground between his teeth to gnaw. "But our animals are reared knowing our scent. Can I say for certain whether or not they are confused by my two forms? I don't know. But as we make no vicious movements on what we ourselves depend on for our civil existence, they pay us no mind. We slaughter no more of them than do any farmers. They have no special need to fear us either as laymen or wolves."

That still left her to wonder. "But on a full moon night..."

A scowl flashed across his face as he offered her bread. "No, not then. When the moon is full, we barely recognize ourselves for what we truly are."

Gerwalta took a step closer, broke off a small piece from the loaf for herself, and gave the remainder back. "Lupines?"

Herr Baron shook his head. "Men, Fraulein. We begin and we end as men." Spinning, he took to the road with a vigor that forced her feet to move swift in time. "A fact I dearly hope that Stephen recalls."

# FIVE

She slowed him down, and it was becoming annoying.

When Gunda Faust had given Andreas permission to leave the forest and chase after Stephen, he wondered if his predecessor's condemnations of the Matron had been misguided. If she could so easily grant a petition that took not only a wolf, but the konigswolf himself, out of her jurisdiction, surely she was a woman of civility or, at the very least, practicality. But when the proviso of an escort had been added, and who that escort was, Andreas knew that Gunda Faust was the type of Matron to add insult to injury and sell it as a blessing.

Fourth daughter to the Matron was a position no wolfsretter would envy. Gerwalta Faust had never even been out the to packlands, let alone been trusted to police any of his pack. Certainly, Gerwalta would have trained in combat, and being righteous she'd have control over silver, but the role of a fourth daughter was primarily diplomatic and, for lack of a better term, *domestic*. The youngest Faust was hardly better than one of Andreas's breeding sows. She'd be married off to an ally or potential enemy soon enough, likely a distant cousin who'd assure the Red bloodline wouldn't dilute. There her role would be to procreate, and to listen. Forget love; wolfsretter didn't consider matters of the heart in their matchings. While lupine pairings could have political aims, at least the mating bond assured that the relationship between husband and wife was one of joy. Fraulein Faust's future was one of disregard, utility, and indifference.

It *almost* made him feel sorry for her.

Then again, she was trudging along at such an intolerable pace...

"Are you ill, Fraulein?" Andreas spoke over his shoulder.

Gerwalta stopped and stood straight as a rod. *With the rod of indignation running up her backside,* as his mother would have said.

"Of course not."

Andreas stopped, turned on heel, struggled to keep his voice tempered. The last thing he wanted to do was suggest to this untested wolfsretter that he had any bad intentions where she was concerned.

"Each of your sisters—even your brother—are able to keep apace of me even on a full moon night. Being of the same bloodline and education, I would think your capabilities equitable. Yet, here we are, two days into our journey, and you appear to be slowing, even though we are walking down a well-worn road, not careening about pines and rocks all around the *Schwarzwald*."

Conflict warred in her features, as though she were equally relieved and insulted that he should broach the subject. Finally, after a moment, the lines around her jaw loosened and she let her arms fall to her sides. "There is some matter of my boots."

"Aye?"

"They were new only last week, and not worn in a manner befitting a long journey."

He took two steps nearer, pleased to see she did not retreat this time. "Are you telling me, Fraulein, that your *boots* have not been conditioned for endurance? That if you need not trudge in them, you may speed your feet?"

"It is not my mother's intention that I should be fielded. What are... Folly, wolf! Folly! You put me down this instant!"

Her tiny fists could sure pack a wallop. Lack of training or no, her blows landed on his back with the full ferocity of her breed. If she had actually intended him mortal harm, his back would well be broken. As it stood, he'd be black and blue from this temper tantrum of hers, but the amusement he drew from swooping up the wolfsretter and throwing her over his shoulder balanced out his pain.

"Fraulein, I am doing what I can to hurry along our journey. We both wish it over as soon as can be had."

"If you do not release me, *your* journey will be at an end. How dare you manhandle a Faust!"

"Have you no interest in seeing out this task with haste?"

"Of course, but—"

She huffed when he put her back to her feet over the rise of the next hill. Before she could manage to make meat of their faceoff, he drew her attention to the sight laid out in the valley below them. "Do you see the village?"

The confusion of such a question turned her from her ire. "My eyes are every bit as good as yours in the day."

True, if annoying to think they were equals in any way. "We are at the edge of the forest now. Up until this time, I have been able to follow Stephen's scent."

She blinked. "But he was two days ahead of us."

Andreas drew his eyebrows up high. "Have you not detected his scent ere we've traveled? Or is your nose not as good as mine, day or no?"

"I…" Gerwalta's eyes closed as she inhaled, pulling the aromas of the glade deep into her lungs. Her tongue clicked the top of her mouth as though she was sampling a taste, and Andreas wondered if his wager, placed on his good humor that he could give her arrogance a comeuppance, might not pay out after all.

Then, the wolfsretter's eyes flew open. Gerwalta huffed as her muscles went taut. "There is no scent of lupine here. Other than yours, which turns my stomach!"

Andreas grinned. Oh, he was enjoying her anger a little too much.

"If you are doing this to mock me then—"

He pressed a finger to her lips, stilling her rebuke. "It was only idle curiosity, Fraulein. It is not often I am able to communicate so intimately with one of your kind. I'm eager to partake what lessons I can."

"Nothing *intimate* shall pass between us." She bore her teeth, and in doing so, forced a curl of confusion over the konigswolf. "Except, perhaps, a blade."

"Injured pride is hardly a slay-worthy offense." Andreas dropped his hand and reclaimed his thoughts. "In any case, his trail here ends.

Stephen didn't proceed on foot from here. Either he begged a ride on someone's cart, or was provided with a horse."

"So close to the village?" He saw the threads of theory weave behind her eyes. "If his stamina is anything akin to yours, it seems unlikely he'd waste good coin to secure a ride for such a short distance."

"My thoughts as well."

The wolfsretter balanced her chin on a fisted paw. "Whoever provided him assistance must have been expecting him. Someone with an interest in encountering him *before* he made it as far as the village. Though, to what end?"

"Stephen was my middleman for brokering the pack's goods to market. He may have had contacts in a town such as this, friends willing to offer him a night's rest. But who? At some point, he must have tread ground again, but even such a small village has many possibilities. I'll have need to scratch around a little, and that will take time. As you cannot help in this, I propose we find an inn for you. Maybe you'll be more quick-footed with a few hours rest."

She ground those very same teeth, but he could also see the battle behind her eyes. She *was* tired, and accustomed to sleeping in luxuries of which he could never dream. The past two nights they'd bedded in the cradle of nature. The thought of a proper bed on which to rest her weary body must be far too tempting.

Gerwalta's eyes dropped to the ground. "If we must."

She remained tight-lipped after that, until, outside the village's small inn, Andreas paused, leaning down to a boy of perhaps eight or ten years, engaged in some sort of game involving sticks and rocks.

"Have you labor to offer, child?"

The brown-haired boy popped up at that, rubbing a sleeve over his besmirched forehead. "Yes, sir. I can carry messages. I can tend horses. I can even see to provisions, such as Unsbach can offer."

The konigswolf drew a pfennig from a sack tied at his waist, before depositing it in the wee lad's hand. "You'll wear the lady's boots and walk about town in them to break them in."

"He'll what?" Gerwalta's indignation returned, and with it, the increase of both pitch and volume in her voice. "I am not giving such quality leather over to a village pauper! These boots came all the way from Mainz!"

"Unfortunately, not on someone's feet, or we'd not have this problem." He pushed Fraulein Faust into a chair that sat outside the inn. "Off with them. When we continue, I'll not have your sore feet slowing us down anymore."

She hesitated only a moment more, finally letting go her objections for practical truths. "It will hurt *his* feet, though," Fraulein Faust said, pulling off first the left and then the right boot. "And they'll come up over his knees. How will he walk?"

"So concerned with the comfort of the laity, now?"

They could use that word here with freedom, at least, for the wealthy were known to refer to the common folk that way at times.

"I am concerned for any creature that undertakes a discomfort in my stead. It gives me a certain level of responsibility to return the gesture in kind."

Andreas disguised his smile with a quick turn, proffered boots in hand. The boy put them on posthaste. Indeed, the result was comical, but as he trudged off to keep up his end of the transaction, Andreas knew it had been a wise decision.

"Then you give him the additional pfennig from your purse ere he returns."

By the time Herr Baron returned to the inn and Gerwalta sensed his approach, the sun had already given up the sky.

In his absence, her lack of utility burned soft embers, every hour left useless adding fuel. *A short tarry*, he'd said. It had been an entire day and then some! By the time the lupine passed into the room he'd arranged for her, Gerwalta burned as red as her hidden cloak.

"Where in the Lord's green kingdom have you been?"

The irritation crashed into him, actually making Herr Baron step back. The konigswolf, however, proved capable of reciprocity. He dropped the bag lugged over his shoulder to the floor and let loose his reprove.

"Where do you think? I've been sniffing every alley and byway, tracing Stephen's trek, while I've graciously allowed you to rest your delicate frame here — and all on my pfennige!"

Gerwalta pushed herself off the bed and grabbed the bag of coins normally tied at her waist. "As if I could not have paid!"

"No, you could not have, for you are a woman."

Red became molten. "How dare y—!"

His massive hand pressed against her mouth, silencing her as he negotiated the closure of the door with his foot. She should have drawn the silver grafted to her torso out and conjured a blade, but injuring the wolf would have caused the same difficulty he must have been seeking to avoid now: unwanted attention. Instead, Gerwalta recognized the need for diplomatic engagement, in lieu of more violent pursuits. She closed her mouth and softened her repose. When Herr Baron seemed certain she wouldn't bite, he lowered both his hand and his voice.

"We are no longer in the *Schwarzwald* and the dominion of Schloss Wolfsretter, Fraulein. This is the world of the laity, and here, a woman of good social standing does not let a room at an inn with a man in tow unless she is a very certain kind of woman, and he, a very general sort of man."

Thinking out the implications, she realized what it must mean. "How precisely did you put our names to the register, then?"

He grinned. "Mr. Wolfe and wife."

When she burst out laughing, Gerwalta wasn't sure if it was because the idea of lupine and a wolfsretter was so ridiculous, or that the false name he'd given hardly did much service in obfuscating his nature. Confusion stood between them for only a moment, before Herr Baron threw back his head and joined her.

"Now that cooler heads have prevailed," Andreas continued, "I would tell you of my findings." He held out a hand to her. "Are you hungry?"

She hesitated a moment, staring at his fingers as though they might nip her. But then, a brilliant thought struck her that if plied with ale, the wolf may dispel the ways of his kind to her more freely.

"Quite." Gerwalta slid her hand out from her costmary leather gloves, and gave her bare fingers to the wolf, allowing him to pull her toward the door. "Feed your *wife* well, Herr Wolfe. A wolfsretter left unsatisfied is a dangerous thing."

Gerwalta had not the keen ears of her foe, but they still bested those of the laity. She didn't miss, therefore, how Herr Baron's pulse quizzically quickened, nor miss the darkness in his eyes when he turned back to her. A queer pulse emanated from her belly into the sacred parts of her frame, a longing to tighten her grip on his fingers that didn't have a rational purpose. Even without the ability to see herself, she knew her innate powers had been called upon, and didn't doubt that her eyes gave off their faint silver gleam.

"Herr Konigswolf, if I have offended you in saying something foolish—"

"No." He shook his head, crossed to the door, and opened it. "You said nothing wrong. I only listened erroneously." He looked at her feet then, as they stepped into the hall. "The boy returned your boots already?"

"Yes, though do you know what that clever boy did?"

"No, what?"

"He filled them with hay and put them on a cow. I had decided to be angry with him, but the hay absorbed the odor and the boots are now so much more comfortable. It was a brilliant idea, Herr Ba... Herr *Wolfe*."

He grinned at her on the end of his arm. "I shall mark this day in my memory of when I received a compliment from one of your kind. And the pfennig?" he continued. "Did you give him one, or should I find him out and pay up?"

"I gave him two."

"Two? Why?"

"Well, the rate, I figured, was for a pair of feet, and three pairs ended up involved in the transaction. He seemed most pleased."

Herr Baron turned his beaming gaze to the ceiling. "No doubt."

The innkeeper greeted them with a loaded smile, one Gerwalta read into easily. He saw them as newlyweds, lovers who had no doubt just come from their marriage bed to catch a nibble. Gerwalta found herself blushing, despite having no cause.

Their hosts stayed only long enough to tell them what the larder could offer, and to receive their request, then skittered off. Within moments of their food being set before them, all the awkward spirits drifted away. Both made due with stew and crusty brown bread, grumbling even as they did that fresh meat would have been the best salve for two and a half days on the road.

"So your search for the trail?" Gerwalta asked when again she felt they could speak with some measured liberty. The other patrons of the inn, likely weary from a full day spent traveling, took to their beds, leaving them alone by the fire. "Was it successful?"

He waved a hand dismissively through the air. "I found his scent in a few places, but only a step or two, as though he avoided touching anything except when unavoidable. Likewise, I could find no trace of his scent on any path leaving town. Either he's still here – which he is not, as I would be able to sense *and* smell him – or he found a way to mask his trail when he departed as well."

She looked to the empty bones of the fish still setting on someone else's table. "How likely is that?"

"If he is traveling by coach or by horse? Not difficult." Herr Baron paused to draw drink. "But it still prompts questions. In whose coach, or by what horse? I suspect we'd find his scent further up the road if we were to investigate, but there is rain tomorrow. It will wash away any evidence of his footfalls in short order. We wolves will ride short times in a cart or mounted, but it's against our nature. We are compelled to stalk ground before too long."

"So water can mask a scent?" There was a piece of knowledge that had not been passed to her. Gerwalta pointed to his left. "Where do you suppose the innkeeper acquired such fresh fish?"

"I'd imagine from the local fishmonger." The wolf chuffed at her seemingly distracting question. "After all, there is a river that runs through town and—" The realization made his eyes bright. "The river."

Gerwalta grinned. "He must have taken a boat, mayhap specifically because he knew you'd be tracking him."

Andreas muttered an oath. "I don't know which disturbs me more, Fraulein: your summation of my brother's actions, or the smile you get when you've figured out the logic of a wolf."

"I may have little experience in policing of your pack, but I am well educated in lupine nature," Gerwalta continued, almost believing she spoke the truth. "The only question that remains, then, is, once he reached the river, did he head east or west?"

"East." The quickness and surety in his voice left no room for doubt. "I overheard someone speak of it today; the emperor's court is on the move again, many of his retinue having passed this way not too long ago en route to Nuremberg. His lady love travels with the court, so shall he pursue them. The quickest way for us to catch him up is to travel the same way."

"We'll not catch a boat this night." Gerwalta stood, dawdling over to a basin to wash her hands. "We'll need to wait until morning. After being about all day, you'll have want of rest, even if the moon has risen."

"My inner wolf wishes to say he can endure, but our journey is long, and pride will not speed it." Herr Baron, too, took to his feet. "I would say that you should make use of the night for your own purposes, but again, here, among the laity, I wonder what that might not suggest."

"I'll remain in the room. My mind can find occupation, even when my body cannot."

# SIX

The innkeeper could have signed his own execution papers.

When they'd set off on this trip, Andreas had had no doubts about the troubles traveling with a wolfsretter would bring, the least of which was normalizing the intrinsic feeling of her proximity. The pull in the base of his stomach when one of her kind neared was born of an ancient power, one meant to warn a wolf of danger. The longer he kept company with Gerwalta Faust, the more he feared the familiarity, and failed to feel compelled by the immediate threat she represented to flee.

One thing he had not anticipated, however, was the need to defend the lady's honor. As the innkeeper took Andreas's coin to settle for the extension of their room, the scent of the man's arousal setting eyes upon the young wolfsretter, coupled with honeyed eyes and a whispered suggestion of how the blankets could be removed if Andreas had a better way of warming himself through the night, put the konigswolf on edge of taking his fur. How easy it would be to rip away the man's throat, but then, how would killing this laymen help him find Stephen?

Despite it only being a few hours past sunset, a time in which he should have either taken his wolf, or passed a good meal with his pack, all Andreas wanted to do when they'd managed to return to their room was lay his weary body down and sleep.

Fraulein Faust closed the door behind them. "You can use the bed. I will tary on the floor."

"That is very kind of you, Fraulein." He placed the candle on the nightstand and went to work divesting his feet of boots before taking off his jacket and pulling his shirt over his head. He'd just managed to pull off his belt when he felt the weight of her stare. Andreas looked up to find Fraulein Faust glaring at him, gap-jawed.

He paused, his hand clutching the brass belt loop. "Is something a matter?"

"You are…" Words failed her, as did her hand a moment later, when it dropped from pointing at him to her side.

*Oh, dear. A bashful wolfsretter. Who would have thought it possible?*

"I am a wolf," he said as plainly as he could imagine, hoping to inspire her indifference. "And I sleep as such. You would know it if you stayed closer when we slept the last two nights."

"I know. That is, I don't know. Of course not, how could I know your manner of sleeping, but what I mean to say is…" Gerwalta tapped her tongue to the roof of her mouth. "You are undressing."

Though he couldn't understand why, he blushed. "Of course I am, else I would turn all my clothing to threads when I shifted to fur. Surely you knew this is a preference, wherever possible, to remove our clothing peacefully before we take our fur. What happened to your claim to be well-learned on the nature of wolves?"

Gerwalta continued to stumble for words. "I suppose I must have known, only, I never thought through the implications. I've never… I've never seen a naked man before."

He actually laughed as he finished off his belt and let his trousers fall, leaving him in nothing but his skivvies. "I assure you, we are nothing to marvel at. The lupine form is much more refined. The male laymen body is quite silly, if you ask me."

Her eyes glowed silver, and caught the candlelight as she looked everywhere but at him. "I wouldn't say it's entirely silly."

How foolish of him, to demean the fact that her kind would never know the grace and joy of being in a wolf form. Still, he had a right to his own prerogatives.

"This is the only pair of underclothes I have with me on this trip, and I've no intention of rending them simply for you to retain your eye's innocence. Look or do not; I honestly do not care."

Her mouth fell open and her gaze became unfocused. A moment later, Fraulein Faust broke from her reverie. "Perhaps if you'd allow me a moment to blow out the candle…"

"We both know you don't need candlelight to see me this close in a darkened room."

"But it... *you* will be less distinct that way." Her hands laced over her eyes, and for the first time ever, a wolfsretter beseeched *him* for kindness. "Please, Herr Baron, being here with you is already peculiar enough to my senses. Do not upset my sensibilities as well."

He did not blow out the candle, but what he did do was nearly as compromising. If she was not to sleep, she had no need of the bedclothes. The wolf pulled off the coverlet from the mattress and made himself a cover-up, tucking the loose end of the linen in at his hip bone, before sliding off his underthings effectively out of view.

"Open your eyes. I'm quite proper."

She did, and the look she gave him when her eyes fell upon him... Silver did not capture the brilliance with which they'd shone. All wolfsretter's eyes were capable of glowing, but as brightly as this? Andreas changed his mind. Swiping the candle off the table, he blew it out and collapsed to the floor. He should take his wolf; he'd be more comfortable, but as the darkness fell and Gerwalta shimmied on to the bed to find her comfort, he hesitated. Why? Was it because he'd wished she'd still talk with him, and he could not answer her in a way she'd understand if he were in his wolf? If so, he refused to acknowledge the irrational hope.

After several silent moments, on the edge of sleep, her voice recalled him.

"You must love your brother very much to tolerate me with such kindness."

"Despite what I predicted, your presence is not nearly as intolerable as I feared." He smiled despite himself. "I *do* love my brother, but there is more riding on his return than familial and pack obligation. I need to keep him from wasting his mating bond on a laywoman."

"But if he loves her without the bond..."

"Is a *wolfsretter* suggesting the validity of a love match?" Andreas rolled over, catching the Fraulein watching him through the dark. "I do not doubt his heart, but he and I are the last of our line. If the blood of my konigswolf heritage is to endure, he must take a *proper* mate."

There she found a hold in which to needle an argument. "Or *you* could take a mate. Aren't you already of an age that you should?"

"I'm only three months into my rule, Fraulein, but rest assured:

38

I *will*," Andreas returned, rolling over. "Just as soon as I find a shewolf worthy."

"Are the females of your pack so inferior?"

"No." The answer was as certain as it was sudden. "Do not misunderstand; I am not saying that they lack in any way, nor that they would not make good mates to any wolf. I, however, sense a change in the winds. The age of war is passing; an age of reason approaches. I wish a wife who shares in that understanding."

"The age of war will never pass until the minds of men are stronger than their desires for power."

"Precisely." Andreas wondered if her eyes widened at his concurrence. "Until they become more like a lupine. This is our existence and always has been: the animal battles to dominate our rational human mind, but we are its master."

After a few minutes of silence, no doubt in which she ruminated a retort to reframe lupines as the barbaric, godless creatures she *knew* they must be, Andreas supposed she had fallen asleep after all. Instead, when she rolled over and spoke again, her words reflected rumination on another matter.

"Will you want to fall in love with her first, or just decide she's the right kind and take her immediately to your bed?" Even through the dark, his sensitive eyes saw the blush of Gerwalta's cheeks. "Forgive me, I did not intend to be so vulgar, but I've always been curious about that aspect of your society, and have only ever been shushed and ridiculed for asking."

"I do not believe one's earnest attempts to seek knowledge are ever vulgar, Fraulein Faust."

Encouraged, she continued. "I know your bonding will induce love, but I once overheard Helga chastise your kind for wishing to fall in love *before* dedicating to the bond. It seems a foolish expenditure of the heart on something guaranteed by the deed."

What drivel these wolfsretter spoon fed their young. Though if doomed to an arranged marriage to enhance the power of the bloodline, he supposed it did have a certain ring of logic. Still, he could sweeten the truth to counteract their poison.

"Love is not the only need for a lifetime of happiness. For

that reason, where possible, we encourage a meeting of hearts before a meeting of... *other* parts of the body. Yes, when I find my mate, I will love her exclusively and excessively—even before we give each other our mating bond. I do not want to dominate my mate. My queen will be able to read, write, conduct diplomacy, and be my equal if not my better."

The pillow Gerwalta held to her face failed to silence her laughter.

"What is so silly?"

"What you're describing is a wolfsretter, Herr Baron."

Embarrassment struck him to his core. "I said no such thing."

"Mayhap not intentionally."

"Certainly not. Beyond the obvious, a wolf could never be *with* a wolfsretter; *she* would never accept me to be *her* equal." He measured the wisdom in sating his curiosity but rationalized his boldness in the fact that he'd likely never again have such an opportunity. "And what does a wolfsretter desire in her future husband?"

Her tone flattened. It was as though Gerwalta were repeating back lessons drilled into her memory by the silver tip of her mother's blade. "A wolfsretter desires nothing. Desire begets passion, and passions misguide the soul. A wolfsretter is paired to ensure the strongest progeny, and to consecrate bonds with other clans. My mother will choose my mate, and I will honor whomever she deems appropriate."

Andreas refused to yield to sleep lest he speak his mind, even if through a yawn. "You will not die alone, but you will not live happily."

"Because my marriage is set before me, a thing done?"

"Yes, *precisely* because of that."

"Is it any different from what you're planning to do to your brother?"

The truth slapped him hard, but a king wolf knew the need to make such decisions were merited. Besides, it was not an apt comparison. "Yes, I will force Stephen to wed, but the mating bond ensures fealty and love follow."

"Then what is the point of having a heart if it is forfeit to the actions of the marriage bed? Why bother with romance at all?"

"Forgive me, Fraulein, that I do not know a better way to put this, but it's because the hunt is a hell of a lot of fun."

Gerwalta scoffed. "Fun? Whatever does that have to do with marriage?"

"For your kind, little, it seems." He pulled the sheet up over his chest. "Sleep, now. I think we've reached the end of our understanding on this subject, and you would not like it much if I were to teach you."

Only, as he fell into slumber, part of Andreas couldn't help but wonder if Gerwalta, in fact, *would*.

# SEVEN

A wolf was near.

Gerwalta awoke with a start, and only in having done so, did she realize she'd dozed off at all. Could it be Herr Baron rousing her instincts, some aspect of her nature triggered by the fact that she'd been asleep? A moment more of consciousness, and she had her answer. This was a different wolf, its energy tinged with anger. Hatred. *Regret*. She'd have asked the konigswolf if he could illuminate the situation, but given the weariness with which he'd return to the inn, Gerwalta behooved stirring him.

Not to mention, as she looked at the pile of man and linen on the floor, one very naked leg, concealed just in the nick of time by the sheet he'd wrapped himself in earlier, stuck out. Didn't he say he'd take his wolf to sleep? Did a lupine shift back to his lay form whilst slumbering, the way they were said to do after death? More questions to save for later.

The proximity of the second wolf remained unchanged for several minutes as she sat in the dark, listening for movement. Either he, too, was asleep—unlikely given the nocturnal nature of one who had *not* spent the day canvassing a village for the scent of a missing packling—or he lay in wait. Only, in wait for what, and who exactly was he?

Gerwalta slipped on her boots and managed to make her escape seamlessly. Taking a moment in the shadows, she summoned her cloak, the red cloth cascading down her shoulders and enveloping her from head to toe. It was better like this; anyone she'd encounter would need to look closely to know for certain if she were a man or woman.

A short walk from the inn, her silver eyes turned on a figure lurking near a cart. One breath in, one breath out...

He bolted.

Empty streets in the wee hours of morn let them both break speeds that would make members of the laity dizzy. The wolf crossed the river via the footbridge, the common square, and soon made the edge of the forest. Even as the trees thickened and the wolfsretter weaved, he managed to stay one step ahead, then two, then more. Soon, Gerwalta lost sight. Then, hope fled as well. The wolfsretter leaned against a tree, racing to catch her breath, when the man's voice found her.

"Leave me be, Red. I have committed no crime."

She didn't spare a moment to wonder who this wolf may be. Coincidence played no role in the supernatural world. She'd hadn't forgotten her mother's edict, but she would not forgo an opportunity to assess Stephen Baron's plans and motives if present.

"You left the *Schwarzwald* beyond the capacity allotted by the Matron and without the permission of your konigswolf. I could have your hide for those reasons alone, but I will grant clemency if you return to the inn with me unopposed. Refuse, and I'll be forced to take appropriate measure."

"You'll grant clemency?" Stephen laughed. "A fourth daughter who's never even seen the packlands, let alone tussled in a real battle with one of my kind? I am of Asena's bloodline, father of all wolves, you pitiful waif. You think you can best me? You couldn't even catch up to me. We wouldn't even be speaking had I not changed form to face you."

Gerwalta's eyes fell over the wolf. She could not kill him; then she'd have no cause to follow him to the emperor's court. She also couldn't just let him go without displaying the bravado a wolf would expect; they were animals, but not *stupid* animals. Stephen would suspect plots afoot if his escape came too easily.

She must restrain him, act as though she were taking him to face his brother, then conveniently let him feel he'd taken advantage of her to get away.

Gerwalta concealed her silver like a skin, grafting it around her torso, hiding it from both potential thieves and her traveling companion. She called on it now, pulling with her power, teasing its state and shape. The liquid metal obeyed, streaming up the valley of her breasts, pooling down her arm, and melding itself into the shape she visualized.

The chain that formed in her hand was hardly a weapon, but she could use it to bind him.

"Last chance. Return to the inn with me now or suffer the

consequences."

"No, wolfsretter. It's *your* last chance. Release my brother, or the consequences will be *yours*."

Gerwalta wobbled out of her crouch, knocked dumb by the words. "Sorry?"

"You heard me. Release my brother from your hold, or I'll have your throat."

"It's not..." Was that all this was? Some grand misunderstanding? "What reason would I have to imprison the konigswolf?"

"Since when does one of your kind demand reason? Your precious Matron must have known my purpose in seeking Court. I'm certain my brother blabbed that, for he advised me against it. Andreas is a weak king, one who refuses to allow wolves to see out the width and breadth of their potential."

"As king, it is his prerogative to do so. As a packling, it should be your obligation to obey."

"If Andreas truly wanted my obeisance, he'd need only invoke my heeling, and I'd have no choice but to comply. Instead, he sent me forth in the passion of his rage, only to regret his decision if your precious spit of a mother learned what I intended to do. Now, Gunda Faust's proxy uses my brother as her bloodhound to track me down."

Gerwalta knew a wolf, separated from his pack, began a rapid fall into madness. Had Stephen's senses become so addled in the space of two weeks?

"You've been misinformed. Your brother came to *us* looking for help."

But that wasn't why she was really here, was it? Andreas merely sought permission to go himself *alone* to retrieve his brother. Her accompaniment had been her mother's condition, one for which the wolf had not been at all eager.

Stephen spat. "Why would a lupine need a wolfsretter's help? Once we are free from your yoke, it is wolves who will save this land."

That threw her for a loop. "What are you talking about?"

44

"Vampires." Stephen pointed behind her, as though one might be standing right behind her. "They have allied with the Ottomans. Openly."

"That is a matter for slayers to discern. Vampires attack neither your kind nor mine."

"The world is changing, Fraulein. We must ally ourselves with the laity, or die at the fang."

"Enough nonsense!" Gerwalta suddenly belted out, resuming her fighting stance once again. She fought the instincts telling her the wolf spoke the truth. Hadn't her own mother suggested vampire involvement on the eastern front? "You've exhausted my tolerance for prattle."

"Oh, it's not prattle. I only felt it my obligation to tell you why I am willing to bring down the wrath of the House of Red by killing you. If werewolves are to survive, we must align against the true enemy. Your kind has become no more than a distraction. Goodbye, Fraulein."

As quick as a clap of thunder, he retreated into his wolf, rippling with fur and fang. His pure silver fur was interrupted by a distinctive patch of brown fur behind his ear. Stephen's size overwhelmed her; she couldn't have anticipated his magnitude relative to his laymen frame. Massive, vicious, snarling, and powerful, he charged at her. A wave that would crush her. A storm that would kill her.

Gerwalta turned to run, but three steps in, the earth rose up to meet her back, knocking both wind and reason away. Colossal paws pinned her to the ground. The chain! Where was the chain? Her hands in his maw, every ounce of her strength went to pushing back his assault. If only she could turn her head and see the silver, then she could reach out to it and...

And what? Wrap it around him? His fur would protect him, unless she was lucky enough to touch flesh. No choice now; she'd need a blade, and she'd have to strike to survive. But then what? Trot back home to a victor's welcome, dragging Stephen's limp lupine form? Her mother would lash into her for failing the mission. She still needed Stephen to get as far as court. There she could slay him, skin him before the sun rose to reclaim flesh, and take the wolf's hide back to Schloss Wolfsretter.

Only, how would she explain to Herr Baron that his brother had been made into a hat or a stole?

And why did she care what he thought?

No sooner had the thought occurred to her than the weight lifted away. Gerwalta wasted no time. She flew from the ground and scrambled for her weapon. It took only moments for the truth to become clear, but it would take a lifetime for the ramifications of that moment to do the same.

The view of him stopped her heart. Regal, terrifying, awe-inspiring, stalwart, massive. Especially massive. She'd never seen a wolf as large or as fierce. Herr Baron's lay form already impressed. Now, wearing a mosaic of tan and russet fur over his back, his white chest rising and falling with each breath, and baring knife-like teeth, no one would question that *this* was a konigswolf. He dominated Stephen, making his younger brother seem no more than an insolent pup.

Silver pooled in her hand for one brief moment, the chain collapsing in on itself before obeying her command, taking on the form envisioned in her mind's eye. Where there had been links, now there was a sword, one the length of her arm and sharp as an Archangel's blade. Gerwalta drew back her arm, ready to assault the smaller of the siblings should the konigswolf gain too much of an advantage. No longer in fear of her life, the grander scheme snapped back into place. She needed Stephen to get away, needed him to lead her to the imperial court. Fate balanced at the end of her sword as Herr Baron pinned his brother to the forest floor.

*I'll throw my blade and injure the konigswolf,* she thought. *I'll claim I was aiming for Stephen, that I thought the battle would swing the other way. An accident. An unfortunate mishap. Maybe if he's hurt enough, I can convince him to allow me to continue the pursuit alone.*

A good plan. A simple plan. An *efficient* plan.

But her hands refused to obey the order to throw, even as the konigswolf's maw latched on to Stephen's exposed throat. Or did it? No, Gerwalta realized. It was merely a symbolic show of dominance, proved further when Herr Baron hesitated. Stephen's neck was exposed; Herr Baron could end him there, ripping his throat away with his dripping jaw. A wolfsretter would. So why didn't *he*?

Suddenly, she understood. Emotion had gotten the better of him. He was not pure animal, for if he were, the fratricide would be complete.

46

Andreas hesitated *because* he was not an animal.

As did she, because she did not want to be one.

The momentary reverie into which she allowed herself to slip was all it took for peril to take advantage. Stephen's body writhed, somehow managing to set the konigswolf off balance. In a moment, their roles had reversed, and Gerwalta suspected Stephen would not stop himself at a mere display.

Gerwalta drew back her weapon, aimed for the smaller wolf's heart and...

Collapsed to the ground as Stephen Baron threw the entirety of his weight backward.

"No, Stephen, no!"

Only fragments of the remaining conflict came into the line of sight. Andreas, in his lay form, using his body as a battering ram, knocking the attacking wolf from her. The sounds of guttural grunts and ghastly growls. A curse the king let out, begging his brother to come to his senses. The breaking of twigs and shifting of earth as the wolf readied an attack. The feel of the silver in her hand as she pulled her arm from the ground, readying a strike to save the wolves from destroying each other.

The press of the king's weight as he placed himself between Gerwalta and death, and one final yip.

By the time she'd come to terms with what had happened, Stephen had made his escape.

Andreas remained.

Naked.

And laying right on top of her.

He held both her hands over her head, even as the silver she still gripped rubbed across his thumb, scorching its likeness into his skin.

"How dare you?" Even with the voice of a man, he still seemed to growl. "How *dare you* try to attack my brother?"

Gerwalta employed all her strength, thinking to kick the man atop her off. Herr Baron, however, anticipated her next move, and straddled her at the hip, pinning her down, limiting her leverage. Good thing her cloak had bunched up when he toppled her, or she'd be looking directly at his wolf's bane.

"What better way to award his disloyalty than to end him?" she pressed. "You were only attempting to do the same."

The corners of his mouth quirked up, though not in a way that made his grin look gleeful. Rather, it looked garish.

"Attempting the same?" He laughed with bitterness. "I was protecting *you,* you insolent, arrogant wolfsretter. Stephen was trying to kill you!"

The claim stilled her body, though it only propelled her mind forward. Herr Baron could not have been near enough to hear Stephen speak the words, could he? "How did you know?"

"Because we still speak words you cannot fathom. Our minds remain sentient." His grip loosened slightly when the threat of her giving chase abated, and though he drew back his hands and released her wrists, he still did not remove himself from her person. "He was downwind on the river when we arrived today. He returned thinking you had somehow taken me prisoner, only perpetuated when you stalked out in the middle of the night without me at your side, for what right woman would venture into the dark of night without a chaperone unless her fellow traveler was held under duress?"

"That's silly, a wolfsretter female is not a..."

"Wolf!" Andreas cut her off. "Fraulein Faust, your Matron has done you a great disservice. So concerned was she in raising a bride, that she forgot to educate a warrior. You are all passion and fury, without any discipline or wisdom. The first rule of defeating your enemy is *sympathy* not *apathy.* If you cannot think as a wolf does, you will always be bested in conflict, just as you were today. Twice."

He stood, and Gerwalta's chin swung to the left so fast, she feared she'd knock herself out should a stone be beside her. Suddenly, a thought came to her: she could still use these events to her advantage. Did he truly think that was all she was good for, to be a bride? Then that's where she'd manifest his unintended injury.

Even if this plan was against her mother's orders, Gunda Faust had never foreseen the dangers of her traveling with a wolf.

Namely, that she began to see Andreas beyond his fur.

"Hypocrite!" She scrambled off the forest floor, determined to take the level of her eyes safely out of harm's way. "Do not you see what you've done? I could have easily slain your brother, and this whole matter would have been solved. Instead, you'll try to reclaim him as one of your pack, and if you do, the story of how I was toppled will echo throughout the Schwartzwald. How well are my marriage prospects then, if I am a wolfsretter who let two wolves overtake her in as many minutes?"

She turned on heel, crossing her arms over her chest. "It would have done better to let Stephen rip out my throat. Now instead of aiding you in your quest, I must end his by any means necessary."

When he reached for her, a curious pang struck her: a desire to round on him and apologize for her initial misstep, but pride cauterized the wound before it fully healed. Instead, she jerked away and began to find her way back toward the village.

"You must stop thinking we are enemies, Gerwalta."

The use of her given name boiled her blood. "But we are."

"No," Andreas cautioned. "Wolves and wolfsretter are, but you and I are just two people. I had begun to think we were... learning to exist beyond that. Please, reconsider. A woman traveling alone in the world of men is..."

This time, *she* cut *him* off. "Is better than a wolfsretter traveling alongside a konigswolf. I wish you luck, *Herr Baron*, in finding your brother. Best pray that you're able to do so before I do."

And with that, she left.

# EIGHT

Mass served a lupine well—except when in pursuit of a smaller, more agile wolf or when fleeing from a pursuer.

When had Stephen gotten so fast? He made mincemeat of the tightly-covered trees, weaving and bobbing about hill and dale with a ferocity Andreas could not manage. Or was it merely that Andreas had slowed, his steps weighted with irrational worry about what would become of a wolfsretter he despised?

But did he despise her? Try as he might, Andreas couldn't convince himself it was so. His thoughts lingered on their last moments together as, defeated, he trotted back toward the village before daybreak. Had she really been at fault for anything? Other than not waking him when first she'd sensed his brother nearby, for surely she must have, he could not think how. Gerwalta was merely giving in to the instincts with which she was born, following a rogue wolf when it gave chase. Though it would have pained him to lose his brother, she would have been justified in defending herself once attacked. She'd created a chain, not a blade, with her silver. At least, at first. That restraint had earned her some consideration in his eyes.

By consequence or conscious, perhaps Gerwalta Faust was not a typical example of her species.

By the time Andreas had broken from the forest, dawn stretched its rosy fingers across the valley. Without the cloak of night, sniffing out Stephen's trail in his wolf form would be impossible. The konigswolf resigned himself to return to the inn. He'd slept some before he'd awoken, feeling suddenly free of a wolfsretter's presence, but not much. It would be wise to rest before resuming the chase. This was no longer the Schwarzwald; both he and Stephen would be obligated to continue on two feet, not four, and would both suffer from the restriction. One advantage Andreas held was the newfound knowledge that Stephen's mind was already beginning to turn. He'd heard it echoed in his words and thoughts during their skirmish. Reason would soon be unable to germinate in the garden of his thoughts. Stephen would be a creature of pure emotion. Emotion would turn to instinct. Then, with the setting of the third full moon, passion would surrender to the beast within.

The innkeeper nodded to Andreas when he entered. "I'm usually the first up around this way, Herr Wolfe. You must have passed some night to drive you out before dawn."

"Sleep and I do not often break bread at night." Andreas shifted his weight, trying to find comfort in the stolen clothing he'd ripped from a fence behind one of the farms on the edge of the village. "I would take it by the reins now for a spell, though, if you would not object, ere I depart."

"Of course not. Late mornings are the privilege of the newly-wedded."

Andreas paused in his turning. He'd forgotten the artifice under which he'd entered their names in the innkeeper's book. The thought of Gerwalta's amusement at being branded "Frau Wolfe" drew a smile across his face.

Which the innkeeper mistook for humor of another sort. "Cherish these days, boy—the ones in which your wife turns to you with gentle eyes and open arms. Once the babes come and the moons fly past, they become fewer and fewer."

"Babes?"

The konigswolf found himself unable to wrest his imagination before it leaped into its flight of fancy. What would a child look like, if he and Gerwalta were to mate? A boy, strong in heart and in body, but gentle and tender in manner. A girl, with hair like her mother's, the color of the cherry's first blush, and skin that would look like milk in the moonlight.

In a turn of a moment, Andreas's face soured. His stomach dropped as the word crept into his thought, guilt branding his soul.

*Traitor.*

What thoughts were these? A wolf and a wolfsretter? It was more than improper, it was abhorrent! A base daydream that belied some sort of defect in his character. What kind of konigswolf could keep the loyalty of his pack, should he take the enemy as his bride?

The innkeeper reflected the reversal. "Oh, Herr Wolfe. Forgive me! I didn't mean to be overly informal. It's only... Seeing you and your missus reminded me of happy days long ago when me and mine were green in years. I see in the way you two kept to yourselves at supper last evening that same fervent passion. I meant no offense."

"No, there was no offense..." A band of sweat glistened across his forehead. Had he caught a chill? But who had ever heard of a wolf with grippe? "Thank you, Herr Innkeeper. I'll... *We'll* be on our way midday."

Back in his room, Andreas landed on his bed, breathless, dizzy. He was getting sick. He must be. What else could explain such a sudden turn in his humors? Perhaps lunacity, the madness that took over a wolf when too long he stayed from his pack on full moon, was contagious. Perhaps in tussling with Stephen, Andreas himself had become infected, for what else could explain...

Lightning touched his brain as clarity invaded. The room was still drenched in her scent, and nowhere stronger than on this bed where she'd lain half the night. Andreas's body had alerted, his animal instincts rearing at the most inconvenient time. He closed his eyes, pulling her essence from the bed and the echoes from his memories. When Andreas had shifted back to his lay form in the forest and lain atop her, quite consequentially and with no other thought than to save Stephen, mind, but, oh, how it had nonetheless stirred his—

*No!* It wouldn't be done. He was a wolf. *He was a wolf.*

Andreas sat up in bed, ripping a stranger's clothes away. They would smell like her too now, having laid himself down where she'd lain. Departing was no longer something he could defer; he had to leave this place where she'd been posthaste. He *must* rid himself of the illogical pull he felt. The konigswolf rolled his coins inside a cloth and tied it with some twine to a thin iron chain he wore at his throat. Then, he let the animal within him out. He needed to run.

And so he did, out into the hall, and into the commons, and out the door into the street.

# NINE

She arrived in Ulm with little money and less hope.

In the forest, a wolfsretter had little difficulty in moving about. The trees leaned her height and their brush and canopy, cover. Had she a keener sense of direction, Gerwalta would have bypassed the roads and made her way across the undeveloped mountains, lousy with pines as they may be. Reality, however, proved a difficult master. Other than the fact that it would increase the time it took her to catch up to Stephen Baron, there were other issues turning her from such actions. She'd been taught to pray and hunt, but not to navigate, and as Herr Baron had predicted, the open roads—and the men on them—were not kind to a woman traveling on her own.

The first time she'd had to fight off the wretched creatures had been mere hours after leaving the konigswolf. At daybreak on the riverfront, she'd talked with one of the traders about booking passage. Then, right out of the sight of town, he and his three crewmen gathered on her, demanding twice the agreed amount. When she refused, they'd taken it from her purse by force. She'd wanted to fight back. Of course, she did, but Gerwalta also knew the consequences of drawing attention.

When one tried to take of her body, however, she'd filleted him.

She'd barely made it to shore fast enough to find safety. Unfortunately, it came at the cost of most of the silver she'd used to conjure her blade. Fighting time and tide, she'd let go her weapon once in the water.

Gerwalta's hand went to her throat, pulling the last bit of the metal that remained unmolested. The blood-claimed medallion, a gift bestowed by the Matron when Gerwalta had taken rites and joined the righteous, gleamed in the sunlight. The token was considered sacred by her people, a piece of silver only once wielded when emerging from the sacred fires that awakened their gifts, then never shifted into another form again. Blood-claimed in the light of a full moon by the wolfsretter presented it, *this* silver would obey only her.

Gerwalta tucked the medallion back under her shirt. She was far from death.

But she did need to eat.

At least she'd been fortunate enough to come into town on market day. On the edge of the market square, she wished away her red cloak. Herr Baron, wolf though he was, had been right on that matter; it was a dangerous beacon, especially now that she was alone. Moving freely through the streets, Gerwalta may have been any of the local folk if not for the particular fashion of her dress; the style revealed her Black Forest origins.

The smells—not all of them pleasant—assaulted her from all directions. Animals held in crates or pens throughout the thoroughfare cawed, clucked, and grunted. Chickens, geese, ducks, pigs... Even a few goats and one small cow. Supplementing the menagerie were spices, the aromas of dyes used on a variety of clothes, flowers picked in the late blushes of summer... In one stall, freshly baked breads twisted in knots and sprinkled with peppercorns whetted her appetite. On the far end of the square, she found a set of vendors offering baskets, fabrics, and rudimentary tools. The bounty overwhelmed. Back home, it was only her father and brother who went to the Freiberg market the first few days of every month. Her mother had told Gerwalta that a righteous wolfsretter born fourth daughter did not require marketing skills when she'd beg to go. "The purchase of sage and the bartering of beef do not aid in the birthing of children," had been Gunda's exact words.

"Fraulein?"

Gerwalta turned to see a small, round woman wrapped in a gray woven shawl, sitting in a stall offering root vegetables. Gerwalta had never cared for their starchy taste in isolation, but admitted they paired well with mutton and its drippings. What she wouldn't give for a roasted leg of lamb now. Her mouth watered at the prospect.

"Carrots? Parsnips? Onions?" The vendor began to hold up her stock in turn. "A few of these?"

The wolfsretter eyed the small, brown curiosity. Something that looked like the result of an egg mating with a river rock. "What is it?"

"They call them potatoes." The jolly woman rolled the thing around in the palm of her hand. "Not much on its own, but mightily able to absorb flavors, thicken stews... Can even be used as a base for breads and pies. Does particularly well when roasted with meats."

A slice of ham or a slab of beef. Either would make her utterly giddy, but even this meager tasteless thing, this *potato,* was more than she could afford at the moment. "Thank you, no."

She turned to go, but the vendor called out. "Is it because you don't have no money, love?"

The truth ensnared her, an act that the vendor took as well as confession. The woman ducked out of the booth, taking a small sack from a place hidden out of sight. When she stood before Gerwalta, she thrust the sack in her hands.

"Mind, these are all on the edge of spoiling, but a few always get nicked and minced on the way into town for market. You'd want to eat them right quick before they go to rot. Won't be much taste without good cooking, but I reckon it will do you a might good to get 'em down all the same."

"I... You don't need to..." Such kindness as this? Who did these things? A wolfsretter did not ask for that which she needed; she either foraged, fought, or ferreted. Here, without even a humble beg, a woman offered up kindness, compassion, and *food?* These were the simple, evil laity her mother so ridiculed for their lack of civility?

First the manners of wolves, and now the way of men. Why had the Matron painted the outside world for her in such colorless and fallacious hues?

Gerwalta rummaged about her pocket for even a single coin but found none. The medallion's weight on her neck tripled. Surely, for such an act of kindness, lifting a few tiny drops wouldn't be unfounded. And who would notice? A smudge of silver's value far exceeded that of a pfennig or two.

The wolfsretter called on her power as she lifted her hand slowly. Three drops of silver collected into a coin just large enough to pinch between one's forefingers. It would still leave most of the medallion intact, and the small bit she lost would be more than worth incurring debt to a laywoman. Done so smoothly, the vendor didn't realize the magic performed before her eyes, focusing instead on the prize it delivered.

"My word, is it really?" The woman snapped up the offering, raising it to eye level to examine its details. Gerwalta did not worry over an emergence of suspicions; her silversmithing could counterfeit the stamp of any coin of the realm. "Wait a minute, Fraulein. Let me give you some of the fresh vegetables. For this amount, you should get something better than half-rotten throw-aways."

"No, please, don't…" Gerwalta's voice faded as she saw the efforts to quell the laywoman's kindness and excitement came too late. On the edge of the crowd, two men who fit every conception of "highwaymen" she'd heard spoke into their shoulders. Two men who were making plans. Two men with eyes on her and a hand on the knives sheathed at their waists.

Gerwalta thanked the vendor but cut off any further pleasantries. She hid away the vegetables behind a nearby vendor's barrel. She could return for it after she'd dealt with these two brigands. With wizened eyes, the wolfsretter took survey of the scene before her. They wouldn't attack until she was out of sight of the crowded market. Laying arms to her here could lead to others lending her aid. They'd need to wait until she was somewhere they could have her alone.

They wouldn't have to wait long. Gerwalta had no intention of delaying what seemed inevitable. She'd best them easily. They didn't know that, and for the moment, that was a huge advantage.

*I go to town to confess, and I go to town to shop, but never both on the same day.* Heinrich Faust, Gerwalta's father, rarely found himself lacking for an explanation when his young daughter had asked as a child what kept him in Freiburg for three whole days when the market lasted only one. On a market day, few would be inside the chapel.

Gerwalta may be of the country, but she knew how to conduct herself in the church, even if its size far surpassed the modest chapel her family traveled to for holy days in Triberg. To the right of the entry sat the baptismal font; a quick dip of her finger before dotting holy water in the sign of the cross about her person played into the illusion of virtuous intents. The men trailed her, likely scoping the chapel interior for witnesses. She'd managed the feat in half the time, using both a wolfsretter's hearing and eyes to look deep into the shadows.

They were alone, a trinity before the altar.

Lithe footsteps drew near as she lowered herself in a nave dedicated to St. Ailbhe. Stone buildings proved useful when relying on one's ears to also serve as eyes. The smaller of the two men went wide and right, while the larger one pulled a dagger from its sheath and approached her from behind. No matter, their weapons would become hers soon enough. Gerwalta worried not about the odds, but it would require waiting for just the right moment.

Three more steps...

Two more steps...

His last step...

"Bloody... hell!"

Hands on the floor, feet kicking out behind her, Gerwalta pushed herself back, only to shoot up again. Now the larger one's back was to her, the maneuver executed so swiftly, the thug's head whipped from side to side, trying to figure out where she'd gone.

"Behind you, Nico!" his compatriot called out, pulling his blade as well. "She's a devil, this—Oy!"

With a roundhouse kick into his stomach, he doubled over, grasping. No time to gloat; turning on Nico, Gerwalta found the man with his weapon ready, balancing it at the height of his shoulder. He wasn't trained in any way. The position would force him to stab down, at best getting her in the shoulder or chest, and without much control over which.

"Now, now, girlie. No need for all this. We just want that pretty piece of silver you got dangling around your neck. And maybe a wee nip at the body beneath it. Nothing to lose your life over."

Gerwalta steadied herself, lowering slightly to give herself bounce. "And all I want is your dagger."

That made Nico guffaw. "Oh, I'll happily give you my... *dagger.* As will Hans, right after I'm done with you."

Hans let out a wet cough. "I'll give her my own dagger, thank you much."

Nico leaned to the left, peering around Gerwalta. "Not what I meant, you—*oof.*"

*Never take your eyes off an opponent.* Untested in combat as she was, that had been a lesson ingrained into all wolfsretter. The second Nico looked away, Gerwalta drove forward, grabbing his weapon hand and twisting his arm behind his back, forcing his grip to loosen. No sooner had she caught the handle of the blade than she shifted to Nico's weak left side, pushing the tip of the weapon into the bottom of his chin.

"If I press this up here, it won't kill you, but it will leave you without a tongue."

Hans fought the conflict through a tight jaw and jutting stop-and-go movements. "Hands off him, wench, or I'll—"

"Hans, you bastard." Nico sounded on the edge of tears. "Don't you see? She's one of them, like the lord. She's a..."

"A wolfsretter?"

With a voice that froze the nave, the man who'd spoken from the back of the church came upon them silently, undetected. He brushed aside his lengthy red cape to show the long sword secured at his side. A *silver* sword. Noble, tall, his hair was the color of winter hay, and his eyes the brown of tree bark. At his hip, a weighted purse pulled heavy. A wealthy man. An affluent man. For every step he took forward, the two thugs took a half step back. Soon, Gerwalta found herself alone in the middle ground, looking up into the churlish grin of her would-be savior.

Or more likely, the savior of the two thugs she would have momentarily dispatched.

He reached out, his gloved hand finding the chain that hung from Gerwalta's neck and pulling its counterweight into view.

"Your medallion seems smaller, Walta."

Tongue-tied. Gerwalta was utterly tongue-tied. Not a new phenomenon, by any means. The only born son of the vicematron of Ravensburg had always knocked the words of out of her mouth.

Gerwalta palmed the medallion. "Perhaps it is merely that I've grown," she bantered.

Bernard threw his arms out wide. "Come now, cousin. Embrace your kindred."

# TEN

The last time Gerwalta had been so stuffed had been at her elder sister's wedding two years before. What a feast it had been! Suckling pig and quail stuffed with cherries. Venison served with walnuts. And wine! It had been the first time Gerwalta had been permitted to drink, the Matron herself pouring the sweet liquid, telling her fourth daughter that she ought to note her older sister's actions during festivities, so that when she herself wed, the night would not overwhelm. After that, Gerwalta had tailed her sister with a deftness befitting the righteous. When the time arrived for Zelda and her bridegroom to consummate, Gerwalta learned what precisely that word meant, all that wine and food betrayed her, landing in the hedges outside Schloss Wolfsretter's keep.

As leaves sprouted, grew green, then turned red and fell, only to renew again when the snows of winter were reclaimed by the land, Gerwalta's objections too had fallen away, curiosity and a smidgen of anticipation growing in its place. The sounds that escaped her sisters' rooms several times a week didn't inspire fear. She was in her twentieth year, after all, and old enough to take a husband. Every full moon, her body reminded her that it longed for union.

Now, here in this parlor, Bernhard became her full moon, every laugh, every smile, every twinkle in his eye causing a sensation of pinpricks.

"And my men thought they'd take you on!" Bernhard laughed, refilling her glass. "Mind, I was tempted to hold back and see if you'd run them through or merely rough them up, but then I recalled how much their services cost me and I didn't want my investment spoiled!"

Gerwalta threw back her head and hooted. "Good thing, too! I am out of coin and would have had no means to pay you back."

Bernhard's goblet paused on his lips. "How in God's kingdom does a woman who can stamp her own coinage with a passing thought find herself without funds?"

She sat a little straighter, letting the comment roll down her lest she pick it up and be bitten. "I know you're of my mother's mind on this issue, but I have never believed I have divine rights to *other people's* silver simply because it speaks to me."

Her cousin reached down and jiggled the pouch tied at his hip. "Good thing I am, else we'd have no way to pay for this meal and I'd force you to fight the innkeeper to ensure our safe retreat."

"Well, I am stronger than you." Gerwalta raised her goblet in recognition, reviving their mirth. When silence fell upon them again, she finally broached the obvious question. "Why are you in Ulm?"

"I was curious when you'd finally ask." Like a child caught in mischief, he froze. "I'm on my way to Ansbach."

"Ansbach?" It was a well-known town, but not one of any notoriety, and not one where the Ravensburg Wolfsretter conducted any trade of which she knew. "Why there?"

"For the last few weeks, we've been receiving reports of livestock attacks." Bernhard pulled another hunk of pork from the diminishing animal on the table before them. "There is word of a wolf who's been terrorizing the region. It may be an unreported rogue."

Gerwalta's stomach became a stone sinking into her feet, even as she efforted to still her tongue, which longed to ask, *Stephen or Andreas?* Asking would leave Bernhard with greater knowledge than she herself would gain, and the imbalance kept her mum. Besides, how would Bernhard know which lupine it may be, and in fairness, it may not be a lupine at all. Plenty of natural wolves populated the woods of this region. And had he not said for the last few weeks? It could not be either Stephen or Andreas Baron then, could it?

"Forgive me for asking—I don't mean to imply you are not worthy of the task—but why your mother? A woman would be best suited to the last. After the death of your two sisters—"

She silenced her words when pain shut his eyes. Bernhard's mother, Maria Dreger, had sent word to her second cousin's court the summer before. A tragedy had befallen their family. Bernhard was the youngest of his clan, his two older sisters akin in age to Gerwalta's own siblings. One night, they'd gone out to run the standard set of patrols. Two days later, their pack's king alerted them to the discovery of the women's corpses.

"I'm sorry, Bernhard. I did not mean to—"

"At ease, cousin." He held up his hand. "I mourn, but I do not linger in my pain. But to answer your question…" Bernhard held his arms out wide. "I am here because I am a man. My mother or any other woman would track a wolf straight away but would be harassed out here in the open world. They'd defend themselves, of course. Draw blood and even kill, if needed, but that would draw attention, make complications. Mother believed a man could be trusted to hunt down and deal with one vagrant lupine. Luckily, and though she is loath to admit it, I am a man."

"Are you? I hadn't noticed."

He made a great show of sucking the juices of the meat off his fingertips. "Yes, you have."

Heat flared in her cheeks, spreading down her neck. Suddenly, looking at Bernhard became as impossible as looking at the sun. "I don't know what you—"

He cut her off. "Why aren't you married yet, Walta?"

At least that question she could answer without revealing any of her heart. "Because the Matron has not yet decided upon my husband."

"That's a lie. Oh, don't look at me that way. I'm not saying it's *your* lie. She's more than decided your fate, she simply isn't certain you're ready yet. What is holding her up?"

The questions danced on her tongue, but Gerwalta knew how music could mislead. "I wouldn't dare assume. I do not know my mother's private thoughts. If what you say is true, and she believes me still unfit, then it is so. Perhaps that is why I have been dispatched for this task, one that, as luck would have it, I believe is the same as yours."

"You chase the rogue?" Bernhard blinked three times. "There would not have been time for word to carry so deeply into the Schwartzwald and for you to come as far as Ulm."

"I set out from Schloss Wolfsretter a week ago to accompany the konigswolf at my mother's command. We were sent to chase a rogue from the Triberg pack."

Her kin across the table looked about, as though the konigswolf she'd mentioned were just over her shoulder. "I have sensed no wolves in Ulm."

"We were… forced to adhere to our natural inclinations and travel separately. We almost had his brother trapped in a village two days from here, but he managed to slip away. Andreas is not in Ulm. Truth be told, I have no idea where he is."

The use of the familiar name raised her kin's eyebrow and the pitch of his voice. "Andreas?"

"Baron," she quickly amended, as though the invocation of his family name would clear the accusation building in Bernhard's mind. "I use his given name to distinguish him from the rogue in question, who is his own brother, Stephen. Andreas as konigswolf petitioned the Matron to try and recover his brother before he became a danger. My mother granted that request on the condition that I accompany him."

"So, what you're saying is…" Bernhard ran a finger lazily through the air. "…the terror this wolf is causing is *your* fault—"

She choked on the implication, a hacking, guttural noise escaping her throat. "I do not think that—"

"—and that, in a fit of rage due to a conflict with the konigswolf—and I know that the fault *is* his, for he is a wolf and you are *my Walta*—you deserted your mission and left him to his own devices; a most grievous act which will draw your mother's ire should she learn of it."

"How would she possibly learn—"

"And that *now*," Bernhard pushed on, "in order to complete your mission, and gain your mother's favor so that she will agree to our marriage, we will demonstrate our superb partnership in tracking down not only this rogue, but also the konigswolf, and assure they cause no more problems for the laity or for us."

"By saying assure no problems, do you—" Gerwalta cut off, finally taking in the full measure of what Bernhard had just said. "Did… you just… *propose* marriage?"

Suddenly, he wanted to play innocent. "Certainly not. I am a righteous wolfsretter, and loyal to both my mother as well as yours, our beloved Gunda Faust, the fearless Red Matron." He rose, extending a hand in her direction. "Come, Walta. Let's set about finding those wolves. Perhaps you'll be wed come spring if we are successful. Perhaps I will be too."

"You are far too certain of yourself for a man."

"You are far too uncertain of me for a woman."


Gerwalta took some relief when her eyes closed before midday. Sunlight drained her, just as it did any of the dark ones. The sun shone for the laity; the night was for lupines, wolfsretter, slayers, and, yes, even vampires.

After such a bold display by her kinsman, she wondered if Bernhard might not suggest they bed down together. Luckily, he took pity on her weary and beleaguered state, procuring another room at the inn where he himself stayed. He even managed to arrange a bath for her, a luxury indeed. When they reconvened an hour after sunset, the respite had renewed her spirit.

Better yet, for the first time in a week, the scent of lupine did not cling to her person.

"You're traveling like you're a merchant."

Bernhard negotiated a sack of foodstuffs and supplies from one of the last vendors to close down his booth in the market, throwing it onto a cart to which a single horse was hitched.

He grinned at her jibe. "A necessity this trip, I'm afraid. In fact, that is in part why I arranged for the strongmen you met, so they could watch it while I slept in the day. I had not planned to share my true nature with them, but such plans had to be negotiated once they began to question why I'd hired them to guard an empty cart."

The horse's mane felt like silk against her hand, reminding her of a wolf's fur—what little she knew of the feel of it. "A good question. Why not simply wait until you were in Ansbach to see if it was even necessary? I'm certain the markets there are just as able to provide such goods."

"I thought hiring the men near our own Schloss would help ensure they'd be encouraged to return. If I'm unable to get the body of the wolf back to Ravensburg before full moon, it could reveal too much to the wrong people."

Meaning, people who didn't have families within grasp of Bernhard's mother. Wolfsretter rarely looked outside their own communities for assistance, and when they did, they made certain to be discreet.

Bernhard continued. "Mother asked me to return with the body, should the wolf of Ansbach turn out to be a lupine, so it could then be returned to his family for burial."

"And so that no men would discover the creature was actually a lupine come next full moon, you mean."

A wolf would hold his beastly form if he died in it. Until the next full moon, that was, when even his corpse would assume the semblance of a man come sunrise. If skinned, the pelt would remain unchanged. Such furs were prized possessions of Matrons.

Of course, most dead—dark ones and laity alike—did not remain above ground long after passing, but wolfsretter had learned better than to assume a quick burial. The expectation when hunting a rogue, then, was for his body to be brought back to his pack. Once with them, wolfsretter cared little what happened to the remains.

Then, what he said struck her. "Bernhard, what do you mean, 'returned to his family for burial?' The rogue we're after is from the Schwarzwald. Surely, his body would need to be returned there? Or is there a wolf missing from the Ravensburg pack as well?"

His face blanked momentarily, before the corners of his mouth lifted into a grin. "We haven't confirmed he's gone rogue, or simply came to dire ends. Of course, if this turns out to be your Stephen Baron, you're welcome to the corpse. I'll even lend you use of the cart, though you will have to get your own horse." He stroked the sumpter horse's black mane. "Terese and I are old friends."

So a second wolf *could* be involved. Only, if the reports coming prior to that of livestock deaths, neither Stephen Baron nor the Ravensburg rogue would have time to commit those offenses with time for the news to travel back. She also recalled the rumors that had been filtering into the Schwartzwald in the weeks before. What was going on?

For the moment, Gerwalta didn't feel it prudent to share such ruminations with her cousin. It could simply be the consequence of a surge in the natural wolf pack populations. It had been known to happen before.

"If it is Stephen and he winds up dead, I'll force his king-wolf-of-a-brother to draw the cart. Look at this trouble he's caused! Imagine what would happen to us in these days of religious fervor if the Church became aware of our existence."

Gerwalta shuddered, recalling Stephen's words in the forest a week prior. Since, all she had done was to imagine just that.

# ELEVEN

Once he'd calmed down, Andreas realized his folly. The Schwartzwald lay far behind him, and with it, the sanctuary the Black Forest provided. He would have to make his way from this point forward not as a wolf, but as a man, and a man would need funds, shoes, a hat...

Pants.

More than anything, however, he needed patience. In hunting his brother, he had an equal in both cunning and determination. A superior, perhaps. The only advantage Andreas could truly boast was his unparalleled size. Two years lay between Stephen's whelping and his own, but they'd been like twins as children. Even then, both knew they were strong candidates to claim the role of king. Unlike the laity royal houses, the leadership of the pack wasn't necessarily hereditary. Coming from a prestigious bloodline that, if their mother was to be believed, stretched all the way back to Asena, the pack saw both as viable prospects when Ugo Kroner passed.

It was up to Stephen and Andreas to take fitting mates, to father strong pups, and to carry their family's legacy into the future. Being king would aid either of them in reaching those goals, but it was in part the pack who determined the wolf that could claim rule in the case of the former king's death. It was only when some of the females turned to questions of the heart that Andreas prevailed. When asked how they would choose their mates, Stephen asserted himself, saying he would take of the pack she who he thought was strongest, and for the good of them all, impel her to be his mate ere his kingship was won, and whelp as soon as possible. Andreas, on the other hand, would seek in his mate a meeting of both heart and mind, and that the shewolf he selected would ask for his paw, for he would win her over with merit, not might.

Andreas won the day, but lost the admiration of his younger brother. Spite at the perceived disregard wove the threads of Stephen's discontent into a loose net. As he dragged weary feet into yet another town on the road to Ansbach, lost in echoes of thought, Andreas realized he'd always known it would come to this. Well, mayhap not this specifically, trying to chase down his brother before the fourth daughter of the Red Matron found him and did God knew what, but a duel, in which only one could emerge alive. After all, both could not be konigswolf, could they?

Stephen possessed an unbreakable spirit, one which did not thrive under another's rule. He demurred when ordered but grumbled about the consequences sure to ensue. Always pushing, always prodding, always trying to tempt Andreas into an argument. He'd finally done it by declaring his intention to wed one of the laity, and a royal at that. Only, instead of allowing their argument to escalate to a king's challenge, Andreas had preemptively disowned his brother and told him to leave.

It was a moment of cowardice and passion, but what was he to do? Kill his only brother? Allow himself to be defeated? Neither fate was acceptable, and now, no other option remained. Either Andreas would return to the Schwarzwald with a reticent rogue tamed and reclaimed, or with a body to bury.

With Andreas's next step came the awareness; the time for fate to determine which outcome would come to pass had arrived. Their gift was also now his curse. The moment he was within a few thousand paces of where his brother would be found, Andreas sensed him. Each footfall weighed heavier than the last. The king closed his eyes. Scented the air. Changed direction. Took three steps. Changed again. Every bit of ground gained increased the pressure he felt just beneath his sternum, an inherent sense that his brother was near.

As Andreas rounded a corner, finding himself in view of the village's only places of business, he found himself fretting. By now, his brother would sense him too. Even though he was downwind, they were close enough now that Stephen could also detect Andreas's essence in the air. Trepidation grew as the distance narrowed, and the instinct of each other's presence increased. Stephen wasn't running anymore. Perhaps he was tired of the chase. Perhaps he'd hired thugs and this was a trap. Perhaps he simply wanted to face down his konigswolf and beg forgiveness. Andreas knew not what lay before him. Hopefully, answers from his kin.

Outside a pub, Stephen sat at a table alone, his hands curled around the handle of a stein. "Abandon this quest, Andreas, before it is too late."

"I cannot." Andreas shook his nerves away, even as he honed

his power, sharpening his words as imbuing them with obligation. "As konigswolf, I demand your obeisance. You will return with me. If we leave tomorrow and make haste, we can be back in the Schwarzwald before full moon."

Stephen's rolled his head in a lazy arc. "I have no intention of going with you, not now or ever again."

An invisible fist punched Andreas's heart. He'd given a direct order, invoking king's prerogative, and his brother had brushed it off like an annoying gnat. A tick in Stephen's smile signaled that they had both come to the same conclusion: the younger wolf had truly gone rogue. Or, at the very least, given his allegiance to another king, though that seemed unlikely. With that knowledge, all matters of pack dynamics washed down the river; Andreas had lost not only a packling, but the last living relative he had.

"Why are you doing this?" the konigswolf asked. "Trust me, Stephen, I do not wish you nor your bride intended malice. I cannot demean her character, for if she were ill natured, you would not have loved her. If it were my decision, I would release your bounds and wish you joy. But we both know that cannot happen."

Stephen scoffed. "Do you really still believe that 'last of our bloodline' hodgepodge? It was all fallacy, a way for our father to manipulate our loyalties to a dying pack."

"I don't care about the bloodline!" Not entirely true, but that wasn't the point right now. "If you don't come back home and submit to me before the pack, you'll go moonmad."

"You mean lunacity? I don't believe in *that* either. An old wife's tale, something shewolves tell their pups to keep them obeying king, father, and wolfsretter. And, ah, yes, the wolfsretter... now there's something a proper king would rally against, and something you're doing nothing about."

The change in direction left Andreas dizzy. "I don't understand what you mean."

"Of course, you don't. You've fallen under their blanket of lies. You think you're actually *konig*, but how can you be a king when you can't even decide the fate of your subjects? Wolfsretter are really the ones in charge, and your leadership? An illusion."

"The wolfsretter are a necessary balance to us, a demand of nature. We can live in the world of men because they are there to push us back if our animal natures overtake us."

"Funny that they don't seem to care if a natural wolf attacks men."

Heat began to gather under Andreas's neck. "If you hadn't gone rogue, I'd show you just how much of an illusion my kingship is by ordering your hindquarters back to Triberg."

Stephen persisted. "What you are, Andreas, is a convenient tool for *them*. They allow a konigswolf to keep the pack managed, but the moment something goes awry—say, your only brother decides to walk away—they send one of their accursed lot to clean up the mess. Then again, maybe that's what you were after all along." He tilted his head and softened his tone. "The Faust girl may have attacked me first, for all you know, but you didn't take the time to search for the truth. You simply rallied to her side and saved her. *From me*. How... curious."

It boiled over now: the rage, the frustration, the refusal to hear another word. Andreas shot to his feet as his arm lashed across the table, taking his brother by the collar and hoisting him into the air.

"Damn it, Stephen! This is not you. You are a good man, not a rebel! Don't make me end you. It will destroy me. Come. Home."

No sooner had his canine teeth grown long then flashes of red and blue caught in the corner of his eye. Guards. *Imperial* guards. And they were pointing their weapons at him.

Andreas read the situation, and knew he'd have no chance. Stephen fell back in his chair wearing a cocky grin that could anger saints.

The konigswolf put together the unspoken truth with ease. "Made new friends, brother?"

Stephen waved his fingers through the air, and the two guards lowered their swords, though stayed near, poised to strike. "Let's just say, the Queen is *very* concerned that I should arrive at court unharmed. She and Ferdinand will be very eager to meet me once he understands the service I can perform on his behalf."

*The queen?* Surely the lady love of whom Stephen had spoken was not the emperor's wife. But that issue was irrelevant. What was of concern now was the threat that had been made.

With two laymen within earshot and focused on his every word and deed, Andreas knew he must paint his thoughts in tepid colors. "If you reveal too much, I will be forced to disown you and repossess your properties. If the Triberg sheriffs need help to enforce my rights as your paterfamilias, so be it."

"One day, brother, you will understand the greater good that I have done for all of us." Stephen nodded, and the guard on his right stepped forward. "Knock him out, but don't kill him. I have a use for him, one that requires his being alive."

As one of the guard's arms twitched, beginning to carry out the order, Andreas's animal mind took over, weighing his options: Fight or flee? Surrender or shift? The consequences of both options played out in the time it took an eye to blink.

A moment of pain as the hilt of the soldier's sword grazed his temple, and then all became black.

# TWELVE

Gerwalta paced by the fire, spinning a web of damnation over the ways of the laity. No argument she could make, however, moved Bernhard.

"But I am a red Matron's daughter!"

"*And* I am three years your senior, and *second* born to your mother's eldest cousin," he countered. "Not to mention, if a member of the laity sees you and I stalking around the edges of the woods, they'll suspect my intentions with you."

The jest had still been partially sincere; the townspeople's eyes would follow a couple of outsiders closer than one passing transient, milling about.

"I sometimes suspect your intentions with me."

"When we are wed, I shall make those abundantly clear. For now, be reasonable. Even though you and I both know you outrank me, there are practical matters which make my going alone best, not the least of which is the storm brewing. I'll not have your mother coming for my skin if you are struck down by lightning. You're not coming along, and that's final."

"But..."

Bernhard managed to press a finger to her lips before she could utter another sound. That simple act, the feel of his flesh against hers, was enough to cut off any utterance Gerwalta may have been contemplating.

He turned at the door long enough to say, "It is fortunate to have found something that renders you speechless. It's a bit of knowledge that may come in use in the future."

That had been hours ago, before the sun had even arisen. How had this maneuver been pulled twice on her? Gerwalta concluded that she'd never again accompany dark one males away from the Schloss or the packlands. Out here in the world of laymen, they got too many ideas.

Finally, as the town clock struck two, the door opened and Bernhard's scent, a mix of worn leather and wine, floated in on the breeze along with him.

"Finally!" The warm bubbles she'd felt from his touch had long since burst, leaving only irritation. "You've been gone for hours. You said you were only going to have a quick look... about... and..."

Gerwalta's ire shriveled in the shadow of Bernhard's engrossing unease.

"What is it?"

His hand went to his head, pulling the hood down. With a sigh, the red cloak faded into nothingness.

"I caught a lupine scent right before sunrise," he started. "I gave chase, but he was fast. So much faster than any werewolf I've ever chased. In the end, by the time I caught up with him... The wolf had already managed to kill again. A young boy, just outside town."

Her hand went to her mouth. "God save his immortal soul." Suddenly, the ramifications of the truth fell upon her. "There is no option now: Stephen must die; that is our law. A wolf may defend himself if attacked by a layman, insofar as he does not reveal his true form, but he may never take human life elsewhere. A little boy against a lupine? There is no defense. When day fades, we will pick up his trail and do what needs be done."

And what needed to be done was allowing Stephen to continue towards his goal of reaching his beloved. Gerwalta still had an imperial court to get to. Stephen was her excuse to get to it. The delay in follow through would allow her time to plot a way for his escape to happen.

"There is no need to track the wolf." Bernhard loosened his collar, pulling his shirt off over his head. Only then did Gerwalta notice the red patches on the front of him. Dark crimson stains where blood had soaked and dried.

"You've already killed the wolf," Gerwalta concluded.

The sympathy in Bernhard's stare faltered. He grimaced. "Would that upset you?"

72

Not exactly, though her mother would be disappointed. No matter; Gunda Faust did not require a spark to set ablaze, and Gerwalta knew she could withstand the fire such news would light. Though as she contemplated the ramifications, the wolfsretter realized there was more to it. Sorrow nipped at her soul. Surely, the boy's death had upset her. But as Gerwalta searched the miasma of her feelings for clarity, she found her concerns turning not to the fate of the rogue wolf, but the brother who would mourn his loss.

Not that she could say that to Bernhard. To show empathy for a wolf—what kind of a huntress would that make her? Not the kind he or any righteous wolfsretter would want to wed. Not that she was overly eager to meet that fate, either, but of all the choices her mother would have, Bernhard was the only one she could envision herself growing to care for.

"Not upset. It's only... I was charged with the task of exterminating the rogue, if the need came about. I worry that my mother will use the fact that a man bested me in that task as a mark against my character," she proffered. Only, that made her think about Stephen's character, and what little she knew about it. Bernhard had never met the wolf; he would know even less. "How do you know the lupine's identity? Did it take its layform and have words with you?"

Her cousin's forehead furrowed. "No, but it is not the possible rogue from the Ravensburg pack. A process of elimination would then suggest it must have been Stephen Baron."

"But what if it wasn't?"

*No doubt word has reached you, as it has my pack, of the recent attacks on livestock in this valley? Natural wolves, of course; all my pack are accounted for.*

"You're quite certain it was a lupine that killed the boy, not a natural wolf?"

"Are you suggesting I could not tell the difference between the two when face-to-maw? The smell alone would prove it if my eyes did not."

True, Bernhard would make no such mistake. That didn't mean, however, that the lupine he'd chased had killed the boy. Nor that that lupine was, in fact, Stephen Baron.

"I need to witness his body with my own eyes ere I sleep. My mind will not be at ease until then."

The disappointment etched into Bernhard's features ebbed. "I did not slay the demon."

"He got away, then?" Ah, hope. She turned, pulling the silver she'd deposited as candlesticks on the nightstand of the shelf and setting it on the table. "I will pick up his trail immediately. There is a storm in the air, and neither of us wants to be in the open when it hits."

A chill ran down her back as Bernhard's hand grasped her arm. He spoke into the back of her neck. "No need. The townspeople caught him."

"Laymen caught... a lupine?" Tension pulled the skin on her forehead taut. Gerwalta turned, finding herself chest-to-chest with her potential spouse—a fact she would have lingered on if not for the confusion stealing her thoughts. "How is that possible?"

"I, too, doubted it. But somehow, through some cunning, they did. They've tossed him down a well, where I was able to catch a glimpse of him. It *is* a lupine, not a natural wolf."

"Put him in a well?" Something about this didn't make sense. "Did he not drown then?"

Bernhard shook his head. "It is dry as yet and plenty deep enough that he cannot escape. They plan to set him ablaze once the coming storm passes and the sun rises."

"Why is there a dry well?"

Bernhard busied himself removing his silver, creating from it a dish that he positioned between Gerwalta's candlesticks. "It's only recently dug. The walls have not even yet been walled by stone."

"Where is it?"

"Outside town, to the west."

Thunder rolled outside, a promise of a torrent creeping its way across the sky toward them.

Gerwalta made for the door. "I will find it, then."

"Whoa, there, Little Red."

Bernhard managed to pull her back before she'd gotten two steps. Gerwalta's eyes went wide as she discovered that, while her thoughts had raced to see that which seemed present but hidden, Bernhard had rid himself of all clothing above the waist. His chest… so solid, so sculptured. Sinew and strength rippled under his skin as he wrapped his arms around her.

"That storm is barreling in. If the lightning finds you, you're dead. Trust me, the well is deep and its walls, clay and mud. The rain will make it too slick to scale. He will be there ere the weather clears."

Despite a voice inside her telling her that the last thing she should do is pull away from his embrace, a twist in Gerwalta's stomach would not ease unless she saw Stephen at the bottom of the well with her own eyes.

"I *must* be certain."

"Gerwalta, I cannot allow you to—"

When she pressed her blade to the exposed skin at his throat, the man before her drained of color. "Why is it you feel you have the right to command me?"

"I will be your husband." He ran a tongue over trembling lips. "Surely my wishes must carry some weight?"

"That does not mean obligation. For now, you must settle with my vow to return before the rain."

She was out the door ere Bernhard opened his eyes.

# THIRTEEN

"Oh, no. Oh, no!"

"It couldn't be. You couldn't have... Could you?"

"For the love of... WAKE UP."

Fire flared on the tip of Andreas's snout, jolting him awake. He leaped to his feet, determined to flee. One pounce later, he fell backward. The burn blazed again, this time on the underside of his front right paw. The konigswolf pulled back his leg, finding a gleaming, metal disk pressed into soft, barren ground.

"Up here, you infuriating... *argh,* just look up!"

His eyes followed the rotation of his ears, taking both toward the cloud-filled sky.

A sky which seemed to be at the end of a long chute, of which he was at the bottom, and against which Gerwalta Faust's red hair fanned around her head, her silver eyes like stars above.

"Change so we can talk, and hurry! There's not much time."

Given the fact that the wolfsretter had just silvered him, reluctance lingered in heeding her demand. As he couldn't make fur nor fang of his current predicament, however, Andreas supposed it was the only option. His bones broke and altered, hindquarters becoming just hind and legs to arms. His laymen form was no favor to him now; as Andreas was rendered a man once more, a driving, terrible pulse pounded between his eyes. A knot on the back of his head rose up to meet his hand.

"Ow!" Closing his eyes dulled the pain. "Where am I?"

"Other than at the bottom of a well, not important." Gerwalta disappeared from view. "Put your back against the wall. I'm coming down and there's not much room."

"You're what?" Was she insane? Into a pit with him? How would she get out? How would *he*? "No, stay!"

She was not one of his wolves; his command meant nothing to her. How she managed to negotiate such a tight space was beyond him. Within moments of the wolfsretter's boots touching soil, she bent over, fetching a metal object from the ground, all without touching him.

Gerwalta shot up, pointing the silver medallion that was the gift bestowed to her people upon their induction into service at his chest. The lip of the disk seared the konigswolf's skin. "The truth or I end you: did you kill the boy?"

"What boy?"

"Was there more than one, then?"

Thunder rolled overhead, but not a muscle in the woman's face moved.

"I have killed no one!" Enough with her inane question. He needed his own query addressed. "Now I demand you tell me where I am and why you're keeping me here."

"You think I put you here, at the bottom of a well to be dealt with later by a bunch of townspeople?" Gerwalta's empty hand flailed to the side. "Since when do the wolfsretter leave justice to laymen? We had nothing to do with this."

A patchwork of memories struggled to weave together through the milky darkness of his recollection. Swimming near the top: a face which brought both love and anger to the surface.

"Stephen!" Andreas growled his name. "He had soldiers with him. *Royal* soldiers. He did this."

Her medallion dropped to the side. "Stephen? You saw him?"

"I did. I…" Her words caught up to him. "Did you say *we*?"

"Gerwalta!"

Both of their heads lashed up just in time to see a handsome

77

face framed by blonde locks and a red hood. Distant storm light flickered, lending further illumination to the silver of his eyes.

Andreas felt every one of his defensive impulses fire. The growl erupted from his throat from behind bared teeth, rumbling its way up the walls of the earthen well, complimenting nature's drums. If his threat made any impression, the blond wolfsretter showed no evidence of it. Gerwalta, however, did not hesitate to display her thoughts, pushing Andreas back against the wall again.

"Your concerns now lie with me, not him. Stephen... Are you telling me he's confirmed rogue, and on top of that, he's under guard by the empire?" Her bottom jaw worked, and Andreas envied the restraint she showed so uncommon to her kind. "And now, he's killed a child."

But the konigswolf still believed in his brother. "If there is a dead boy, it does not mean Stephen killed him. That *any wolf* killed him."

"Are you suggesting two lupines so close to full moon and in a heated debate with each other might not slay an innocent who drew too close to their struggle?"

"I cannot deny the possibility and you know that. But I also know that the world of man faces many more dangers than werewolves." Why had his anger risen, when he himself had just admitted it might be true? "If I can see the boy's body, *smell* it, I will know if his death was from my brother's maw."

"How would I know you'd be telling the truth?"

Something in her gaze, a certain softness or, perhaps, desperation, struck him, setting Andreas on a strange precipice. A sympathetic wolfsretter? One who wanted to believe in *his* better nature? If he allowed himself to look over the edge, he'd fall and suffer the rocks below.

And he was *so close* to falling where Gerwalta Faust was concerned.

"You wouldn't *know*, Fraulein." Without understanding why *he* suddenly felt a need to comfort *her*, Andreas stroked her cheek with his muddy hand. "You would have to *trust* it."

He didn't need his flesh on hers to know of the uptick in her pulse. His ears picked up the sound, reflected in his own, as their eyes met. Gerwalta's lips parted, perhaps intending to rebuke his forward actions, or perhaps because she had meant to, but reconsidered.

Of all the times for animal instinct to kick in, it would be now, wouldn't it? The way her bottom lip quivered, how the swirls of wind that tunneled down the shaft swirled the loose red hairs, the way she inhaled so deftly, he wouldn't have picked it up had he not be staring at her... The touch of Gerwalta's cheek suddenly seemed insufficient. Andreas wanted...

Irrational things. Impossible things.

*Dangerous* things.

A male wolfsretter's bellow from above broke the spell. "Gerwalta, we *must* go!"

As quickly as the temptation arose, Gerwalta's sudden fear subdued it, diverted it, redirected it.

"What frightens you?"

Her eyes shot up. "The storm."

Were her kind such frightened children concerning weather? "It's only a little thunder and lightning."

"Precisely, *lightning*. It's attracted to silver, and silver is attracted to us. Hence, lightning seeks us. Unto death, as it were."

Fear quickened his pulse. "You must get inside."

"I know, only, first we must—Herr Baron, what are you—Herr Baron? Herr—Baron!"

In the space of a thought, the konigswolf wore fur once more, the bottom of the well just wide enough for his paws to anchor. Gerwalta, thrown against the wall by the power of his turning, gawked. When he sunk down, sinking low, it took her a moment to understand what he'd implied. Then, knowing his intent, it took her a moment more to believe it. A lupine was no beast of burden, and one's pride and independence, thorns upon which many a casual gardener had pricked a finger. For a king wolf not only to offer a mount, but to do so for a wolfsretter, was a heretofore inconceivable occasion.

Another demon finger poked across the sky, chased by thunder with such ferocity, both the woman next to him and the man peering down from above called out. Gerwalta trembled, even as she crawled on to his back and pulled on his fur so tightly, he winced. The rain which decided to fall upon them from above just at that moment weighed heavier upon him than her lithe frame. He could not delay; within moments the earthen walls rising above them would grow slick.

Andreas coiled, and then he leaped.

"What are you—" Her comrade's words died, before he bellowed out, "Walta! Take my hand."

Great was the strength of the king, but it had not quite been enough to make the surface. Andreas's claw craved dirt, clung to it for dear life. Under paw, soil shifted, just like the muscles in his back, burning, trying to hoist himself and his rider the last few feet to safety. Gerwalta managed to take the offered hand, and with a tug from the male wolfsretter, she fell forward unto the flat earth. He wasted no time in gathering the woman to her feet and whisking her in the direction of a scattering of buildings just a short distance away. Andreas lost sight as he slipped a little, his maw back beneath the level of the ground.

It should have freed his strength enough to pull himself up, but his body refused to comply. The blow made by the guard and a day of sitting in his wolf must have drained him more than he'd realized. Adrenaline had pushed him to save the wolfsretter, but would he be able to save himself? Andreas looked back over his shoulder, mentally preparing himself for the fall and the impact that would assault his body below.

"Walta, leave him!"

Suddenly, his world turned red.

The cloak he'd been raised to fear? The crimson veil he'd been forced to respect as king? The thing he'd always known was the only enemy capable of destroying him…

Saved him.

"Andreas, quickly!"

He obeyed, taking Gerwalta's magically-apparated riding hood in his maw, as the wee mortal form struggled to pull his massive body free of the well.

"Please, Bernhard, help!"

80

"But he's a—"

"Bernhard, I'm giving you an order!"

Did *she* have command over *him*? Even though he'd known the Matron ran the roost in wolfsretter society, did that authority trickle down to subsequent generations? It must have, for as quickly as Gerwalta demanded it, *Bernhard* complied.

They all ran for salvation the moment their feet hit the ground. Andreas tailed them as soon as he'd managed to get his bearings. Thank god for the dark and tumult, for it masked the light of the moon and any chance a villager could peer out a window and watch a man and woman run full speed into the nearest barn, with the wolf who may have killed one of their precious children seemingly on their heels.

She should run faster. *Run faster!* If a man, he'd have yelled it at her. But Gerwalta suffered the consequences of looking back over her shoulders. It was slowing her. Damn it, could she not feel the sting of the lightning gathering strength in the cloud above? He could, and if it was such a danger to her, she must.

Bernhard lashed open the door, turning on his heel, cycling his hand to urge them on. "Walta, do not worry about him. Just—"

The sizzle. The shift. The crackle.

The bolt.

He had to.

Andreas crouched, pounced, attacked.

And barely got her inside before the lightning found him.

# FOURTEEN

All night and well past dawn, Herr Baron had not awoken.

The smell of charred wolf flesh still permeated the air. At the crack of dawn, Bernhard had preempted any awkward discoveries by accosting the landholder, intending to claim that he and two of his kinsmen had taken shelter from the storm in his barn, and offer silver coins for the inconvenience.

For the moment, their secret was safe. But the cows in the corner of the barn were growing restless, their utters bulging with milk. Soon, the farmer would have no choice but to come, and when he did, he'd see the bulky wolf who'd been in the well the night before, the fur singed off his hindquarters and his flesh charred on the surface.

How could konigswolf sleep so deeply? He deserved it, of course. If Andreas had not leaped at her when he did, the lightning would have claimed Gerwalta herself. Unlike the lupine, she would not have survived. Few mortal things could kill a wolfsretter: a stab through the heart, beheading, disembowelment… These things would destroy any of the dark ones. But lightning? Vampires, slayers, and wolves would smart after a strike, but the wolfsretter alone would perish.

Yes, if she could, she'd have given him a feathery down bed, fresh sausages, and asked if she might draw him a perfumed bath in appreciation. For the moment, however, she needed him to wake the hell up and take his lay form before the villagers discovered their demon wolf harbored in the barn.

A bucket of frigid water finally slapped him into consciousness. Herr Baron's eyes and mouth shot open as he shifted in an instant from animal to man. The konigswolf cursed the sun and all the saints as his head lashed around, trying to find reason in his surroundings. All too soon, the memory of the previous night dawned on his face. Baron spun, examining the injury that had followed him from one iteration to the other. Black and blue blistered skin made up his backside. A shame, truly, for she remembered from her brief glimpse his *backside* had been rather fetching for a wolf. His hands curled around his body, making him wince as he pushed at the cooked flesh. A moment later, his hands circled forward. Gerwalta half hid her eyes as the konigswolf took inventory of his manly endowments, grinning when he found them without flaw. She couldn't help but let out a tempered laugh.

The sound drew his eyes, to where Gerwalta stood in the barn rafters. Gerwalta wondered if he was busy comparing her to the disembodied head of the ox mounted for luck to the main beam, thinking he'd like to make her serve the same fate. The emotion he wore was one she could not decipher.

"Are you unharmed?"

Which was why his words took her so aback.

Her mouth fell open. "How can you ask me that?" In a slight shift, Gerwalta walked off the end of the beam, falling with perfected grace beside the konigswolf. The distance would be enough to injure most laymen, but Gerwalta scarcely made a noise in the effort. She only hoped she had not slowed her descent so very much that he noticed the unnatural leisure with which she landed. "After what you endured, how can that be your first question?"

"Fraulein, it is the very reason I endured what I did." He looked like a statue, a creature of stone which would not move lest she breathed life into him. "Were you injured?"

"No, you... You *saved* me." Something foreign invaded her senses, a pull toward a wolf, a longing to set his mind at ease. But all too soon, Gerwalta's sense of self returned. She squared her shoulders. "But there is still some matter to attend to, Herr Baron. The boy... My cousin has gone to inquire about his whereabouts. You *will* still hold to your word; you will inspect to see if Stephen was responsible for his death."

"Right, then." The chill of her formal tone drove the tenderness from his gaze. Herr Baron coughed once, planting balled fists on his hips and casting his eyes to the floor. "You are certain, then, that I am not responsible?"

"Methinks a wolf who would put himself in the way of such harm to save his enemy is unlikely to have attacked an innocent child who could offer him no threat."

"Is that what we are, Gerwalta?" Boldness in using her given name brought his eyes to hers. "Enemies?"

Why the questions should strike her dumb, she knew not. Before she could muster an answer, however, the barn door swung open and a red-cloaked figure entered.

Bernhard's arms were full, a heaping assortment of cloth, victuals, and something oily and pungent inside an animal skin. Seeing the two of them facing off, he let everything fall to the ground just as soon as he cleared the door.

"Bread and cheese. A paltry meal, but the butcher is part of the hunting party and will not open his shop today. The clothing may not fit you, wolf, but it will have to do. And here—" Bernhard nudged the animal skin toward Herr Baron. "A salve the farmer in whose barn we are standing passed along. I thought it a rather odd gesture, when I mentioned nothing of your injuries, but he bade me make use of it."

Had she really been in such mortal danger that Bernhard would show the lupine kindness in appreciation? Gerwalta grinned, still unclear why that pleased her.

Baron took up the skin and dabbed his finger into the paste, pulling a small sample to his nose for inspection. Gerwalta assumed he'd apply it to his burns once he was assured of its content. *Not... that...* her interest would be piqued by watching him contort his body again, making the muscles under his skin pull and stretch. Instead, the naked lupine grabbed the empty bucket and the stack of clothes and made his way to the cows in the corner.

"Modesty now, Herr Baron?" Bernhard asked. "I assure you, we are both well-seasoned wolfsretter and are unaffected by your natural condition."

For her part, Gerwalta was not so sure that was true.

"Even so..." He pulled on a set of britches that proved to be far too short, even if they did fit him around the waist. "This salve is one used in the milking of cows. Keeps the udders from drying and cracking. This is the use the farmer intended."

Bernhard didn't raise a word of protest, instead turning to her as the lupine found a short stool and set to work on one of the heifer's teats. "I have both good news and bad news."

"Out with both in whatever order you like," Gerwalta said. "It will change the net to rearrange the gross."

The male wolfsretter nodded. "The villagers are laying this attack at the feet of a werewolf."

She clutched her chest. "We've separated from the world of man for nearly three hundred years, and still, they know of us."

"Ah, but that is the good news," Bernhard continued. "Their conception of werewolves and the truth of lupines seems divorced. Nevertheless, it will mean we must be even more cautious as we go about our business here, for the slightest thread could unweave the tapestry."

"What will they do, throw me in a pit *again?*" Andreas grumbled in the background.

Gerwalta chose to ignore him. "Luckily, it seems laymen no longer recall the existence of wolfsretter, and Herr Baron has demonstrated mastery of his animal spirit, so I do not fear any error on his part. Still, we should not linger."

"My men will be ready to leave just as soon as we've had a chance to stop and see the boy's body, under the auspices of our making condolences to his kin. But we have another problem."

She blinked twice. "Yes?"

"When the villagers discovered the wolf escaped, they were incensed. They've formed a hunting party and are preparing to search the woods. I cannot blame them. A child is dead, and they need to take from nature what, in their view, it has taken from them."

"Surely you are not suggesting that we give the konigswolf—"

"No," Bernhard said. "But they will need *some* wolf to sate their fury. Since the other lupine is likely long gone by now, that means taking from whatever stock the local forest holds."

The squirt of milk stopped midstream.

Gerwalta had no time for the sentimentality of a lupine for his natural cousin. She nodded once. "I understand."

# FIFTEEN

A mother's sorrow is sharper than any knife and twice as lethal as any poison.

Even before the door opened, wails rent the air. Andreas felt his knees buckle, the force of memories past washing over the present, leaving his footing pulled in a riptide of emotion.

The rail-thin, gray ghost of a man looked out at them, sneering his words. "What is it?"

Bernhard Dreger snatched off his cap, holding it before him in his hands. "Apologies for the intrusion. Sir, my wife and I were passing through town last night and this morn heard the terrible news. We've come to offer our respects and our prayers."

Andreas couldn't explain why the vein in his temple throbbed at the assumed identity the male wolfsretter assigned Gerwalta. Inwardly, he lectured himself. *Stay focused. Stay silent. Stay in control.* Outwardly, he became aware of the old man lifting his eyes to appraise the wolf in disguise standing behind them.

"And him?"

Bernhard looked back over his shoulder for a moment, a proper acknowledgment that passed quickly. "My wife's brother, sir. He's a simpleton, but a good man, and devout in prayer. Of course, we understand if you'd prefer we left you…"

Bernhard leaned forward a slight bit, and the way the old man's eyes lit up suggested that the young wolfsretter had deliberately let his sacred silver medallion slip into view. A family might turn away others in a time of grief, but a poor village home would not be so quick to let a wealthy merchant's attention go unheeded, no matter the circumstance. The senior member of the household stood aside, inviting them in with a sweep of his arm. Inside, women embraced the grieving mother. The father, nowhere in sight, must have been with those canvassing the woods in search of the culprit.

Bernhard and Gerwalta made a show of giving respects to those in the room, all while Andreas made his way to the tiny echo of a human laid out on the cottage's only table. Someone had covered his body in linen. He'd been washed then—likely to clear the blood away—but it didn't matter. As soon as Andreas dropped to his knees in prayer beside the body, a panel of aromas gave away the truth. The konigswolf's posture was no ruse; he prayed in earnest for the poor victim's soul, adding benedictions for the suffering family, the village, even the wolfsretter behind him.

Before he rose, his whispers besought heaven for one more who hadn't suffered yet, but would. "An eye for an eye. A tooth for a tooth."

A life for a life.

The boy reeked of his brother's scent.

That was not a surprise, however. What *did* take him aback was the marker of a second lupine, one not of his pack.

And female.

Andreas crossed himself as he rose and turned to Bernhard and Gerwalta, both offering what comfort they could to those in mourning.

Bernhard cut off a man similar in age to himself. "Herr Seidel, I understand a hunting party is after the wolf which escaped last night."

The villager blinked his surprise. "You seemed to have learned a great deal in short order."

"It is because of my wish to be of service." Bernhard gave a respectful nod before continuing. "I would consider it an honor to assist. I am a marksman of some renown in Bavaria. An excellent tracker as well. I can fetch my bow from my men at the inn and join the others at once."

None within earshot raised any objection, and several voiced their gratitude. Soon enough, the three of them were heading toward the door, and Andreas found himself locked against his better nature in debate.

Stephen was his packling, his brother, his responsibility. Now that he'd confirmed the rogue wolf's involvement in the boy's slaying, Andreas was dutybound to rectify the situation. But this second wolf? He knew not her situation, her pack allegiance. He knew only that she'd taken several bites into the boy. To disclose another wolf's involvement to the wolfsretter, however, would be to doom a stranger to the...

Gerwalta had said it herself, hadn't she? To the *enemy*.

They paused some twenty paces from the cottage, Bernhard pointing toward the collection of timbered houses just off in the distance. "My men are there. Tell them to ready the horse and the cart. We'll be about our way ere I return."

Gerwalta caught her cousin's shoulder as he turned to go. "Absolutely not! I am not being set aside for a third time to appease laymen expectations! And do not think I'm letting you wander off alone when there is a rogue wolf unaccounted for."

"Stephen will have fled by now," Andreas supplemented. "I have had no sense of him since I awoke in the well last night. If he was concerned with the outcome of what he wrought here, he would have lingered long enough to make sure I was good and framed for his misdeed. He considers me as good as dead."

"Be that as it may, Herr Baron, my cousin is right. The villagers need an offering to account for the life lost. We'll need to reap a natural wolf."

His fists tightened at his sides. "An innocent animal."

"To make amends for the life of an innocent boy!" she snapped back before turning to Bernhard. "I'm coming on this hunt. The sooner we find a scapegoat and offer it up, the quicker we can be. I overheard talk that the hunting party is heading west; I suspect that will drive the animals east. You tend the villagers and keep them hunting toward the river, and I'll skirt the hills and find a sacrifice."

Bernhard shook his head. "And I'm supposed to be any more at ease with *your* going off by yourself under the same circumstances, merely because you are a woman? No, I refuse to allow this."

"Every moment we debate and haver, Stephen gains. This is not a discussion. I have determined our course of action."

The male wolfsretter crossed his arms over his chest, examining his kin at some length. "Woman or no, I do expect a little more deference when we are wed."

"Wed?" The word was out of Andreas' mouth before he could

think.

The wolfsretter turned on Andreas with dueling expressions. Bernhard wore smugness in his features, a bold pride that boasted a snagged doe. Gerwalta, on the other hand, radiated embarrassment, as though her deepest, darkest secret had just been laid bare for the world.

"All is assured except the formalities," Bernhard said. Then, turning, back to Gerwalta, he continued, taking her feminine yet fatal hands in his. "Dear heart, I'll remind you once more that here among the lay, ladies do not head off to the forest to hunt dangerous predators alone."

He couldn't believe what he was saying. Andreas couldn't believe what he was about to *do*.

"She will not be alone." Andreas stepped between them. "I will accompany her. If confronted, she can feign a lady's delicate nature, and I can maintain my act of being a simpleton. But Fraulein Faust is right; we need to be diligent about resuming the road, and I assure you, no matter how good the two of you are at tracking prey, *I* am better."

# SIXTEEN

They waited for Bernhard and a few men who were late to the day due to their chores to gather. Her cousin passed her one more pleading glance, but Gerwalta would not be moved. She responded with a barely perceptible shake of her head. He grimaced, then left.

One man deterred, one more to go...

She spun on the konigswolf as soon as the forest gave sufficient coverage. "I do not require minding, Herr Baron. Stay here. I will circle back after a short while, regardless of whether or not I find a target."

"You will find a target," he assured her. "Your instincts hold with mine. If there is a pack in this forest, the leader will guide them away from the angry footfalls of men. But you are wrong to go in alone."

"I am trained to fight lupines. You seriously think the less intelligent and smaller natural wolf will present any problem?"

He took two steps toward her. "I do, and for the very reason you just cited. You have been *trained,* but you have not had sufficient *experience,* nor enough failures to correct your misconceptions."

The wolfsretter tried to remain focused, driven. She'd need to render a weapon. Turning, she found a fell tree, offering up its limbs. Two branches, thick enough to provide a base to her creation and small enough to be easily swung, each segment about the length of her forearm, would do the trick. Gerwalta summoned the silver woven in threads under her tunic, graphing blades onto the length of wood clenched in her hand.

She pulled the double-headed axes to eye level, examining her workmanship. "Are you suggesting I would be a better huntress if I were a bad one?"

"At first, yes." His footsteps fell soundless as they veered away from the well-worn path made by the villagers into the underbrush. Above, September's autumnal kiss had already brought a blush to the foliage. The floor of the forest, still damp from the previous night's rain, had begun to resemble one of Zelda's many calico cats. "Experience, not imagination, teaches us where our fallacies lie."

"I've also been trained to be a proper wolfsretter wife and mother. Are you saying I should set about obtaining a practice husband to make me a better bride?"

"I'm not certain one would need to go to such extremes to earn some knowledge in that area." He paused. "But have you even ever kissed a man?'

Struck dumb by the question, her feet stilled. When she slowly turned to study his features, she found an earnest man asking an earnest question. "Have you?" Then, realizing the folly of her retort, Gerwalta closed her eyes and huffed. "Kissed *a woman,* I mean. I thought your kind only mated once and for life."

"Fraulein, there is quite a bit of ground one can walk before *mating.*"

*Really?* "So you have, then?"

"Kissed a woman?" His tone held no shame. "Of course, I have. When I am blessed to find my mate, I endeavor to provide her a lifetime of not only companionship, but pleasure. It is my duty to her happiness, to make sure I am equal to the task." He leaned forward, his voice conspiratorial. "Is there some concern that Herr Dreger would be unable to... *fill* the role of your spouse?"

The insinuation and overly familiar nature of his question shot fire up her spine.

Yes, that was the reason. The *insinuation.*

"That is none of your concern."

"It should be yours. At least I know my mate will always be true to me; wolves cannot commit adultery once bonded. At least, not without extreme pain. A wolfsretter, on the other hand..." Andreas crossed his arms and shrugged. "Not that I would be interested, but he is a rather handsome lad, and you would need him to conduct your house's business in the layworld."

How infuriating. How impossible, insulting, improper, and infuriating! "Not that it matters, for the purpose of a mating... a *marriage,"* she corrected as she set her improvised weapons down on a fallen tree, "is security and procreation, not *pleasure.* I am quite certain my... *skills* will be deemed appropriate when the time comes."

Herr Baron leaned against an oak tree, looking smug, despite his too-short pants and the pull of the undersized shirt against his chest. "For Bernhard's sake, I hope so. I've been the recipient of an inexperienced kisser's attempts before. It is an awkward experience. You ought to practice. Get the feel of the cloth before it is cut, so to speak."

"Fine." She crossed this distance to him without thinking. "Kiss me, then."

The wolf went stark white, his eyes falling with a red leaf from above and landing on the ground. "Fraulein, I wasn't implying that—"

"Come now, wolf!" He was at least a hand and a half taller than her. Gerwalta found a rock just a few steps away that would solve that and leaped atop it. "Show me what I supposedly have to gain, if you're so great at it." Gerwalta opened her arms out wide. "For Bernhard's sake," she mocked, "kiss me."

When Herr Baron lifted his gaze again, Gerwalta was convinced the rock beneath her had melted, leaving her struggling to stand.

She'd never known the feeling of being hunted before. Of being the sole object of a predator's intent. Now, she couldn't escape it. The man was gone, leaving the wolf in his place. Baron intended to eat her, consume her, to lick every morsel of meat from her frame and leave her a pile of bones on the ground.

He licked his lips, slowly, methodically.

*Sensually.*

"Very well, for Bernhard's sake."

Six languid, long, lumbering steps from where he had been leaning against the tree, brought him to a place where he could lean into *her.* Only when his breath brushed her lips did she truly grasp that she'd been caught, that she was as good as a doe pinned to the ground, despite her two feet planted firmly beneath her. His arms stayed at his side, even as hers rested upon his shoulders. His eyes drifted closed as his head angled. Despite the leverage of the stone, she was still slightly shorter.

All the anticipation? All the heat that had suddenly welled

within her? It died with the first press of his lips to hers. Nothing. No desire, no shudder, no effect. Other than having a wolf's spittle on her mouth, which hardly seemed a good payoff.

"Fraulein?"

"Yes?"

Her eyes fluttered open, just as he pulled back just enough to look at her. "You have to open your mouth."

"I—Oh! I didn't know. I—"

But he didn't wait for her to stop. Instead, Baron pressed his lips to hers again, and the last thing Gerwalta was, was unaffected.

It was like the heat of her awakening fire, fed by a thousand suns and stoked by five thousand logs. Andreas was the animal, but she was the one driven by a primal nature. Her arms embraced the lupine's head, her fingers running through his hair. Even as his mouth worked hers into rapture, it took a moment for Gerwalta to realize the moan she heard was her own. Then again, his mouth was muting it. And his mouth! What delightful things it could do when not speaking.

Then, just as suddenly as it had begun, it ended. Andreas pulled back, creating a buffer of air between them.  Some part of her took delight in the fact that he was breathing just as hard as was she. Was she as flushed as he appeared to be? The wolf seemed to be positively stunned, as though he'd been knocked over the head with a club. Another step back, and the chill that pressed in on Gerwalta was actual as well as emotional.

He lifted a hand, as though telling her not approach. Only with that gesture did she realize she had been attempting to do so.

"Jesu, woman, are you certain you've never..." Andreas let out a hoot. "That was your *first* time?"

"Of course, it was!" Then, worrying about what he implied, she ran her fingers through a pool of self-consciousness. "Why, was I so bad at it?"

"Bad at it?" The wolf ran and through his hair and grinned. "I assure you, Herr Dreger will find you *more* than sufficient. You nearly *undid* me. You—"

His words cut off at the same moment they both turned.

The rapid *lub-dub* of their hearts was no longer about what had just happened, but what was about to transpire.

Gerwalta scented the air. "Lupine or natural wolf?"

"Natural wolf, of course."

He rounded on her just as he began to pull the rope which had been improvised for a belt from around his waist. Gerwalta had barely reached him to keep the trousers from falling in time.

He blinked at her, confused and visibly amused. "What are you doing, Gerwalta?"

She bristled, fixing her ire on him. "Do not presume such familiarity with me, wolf."

"I know your taste now, *Fraulein*. I think that entitles me to address you by your given name privately, if not publicly. My name isn't wolf, incidentally. In case you forgot, it's Andreas." His eyes darted meaningfully to his lower portions. "I'll agree that they do not suit me, but the pants would look worse on me as a wolf."

"But if you remove them, you'll be nude."

"As I was this morning in the barn, and you made nothing of it then."

*That was before I kissed you,* she thought, but conditioned herself to remain stoic. "Give me a moment's start." When he conceded and held his pants aloft, she turned to grab her weapons. "You can catch up."

"You don't mean to harm them, do you?"

His words caught her dead in her tracks. What did he suppose she'd intended when she crafted her blades? "I don't mean to invite them to supper."

"But they are innocent animals."

"As are you, but there is still a dead boy and the villagers must have blood." Her cloak would help contain her scent and her sound as they tracked, and so, Gerwalta summoned it, welcoming the familiar feel of red fabric against her arms and neck. You knew that was why we were out here. Do not act surprised that I'm following through."

94

He held up his hands, examining them. "Perhaps I should have stayed in the well. Ultimately, Stephen was able to kill the boy because I was not a strong enough king to dissuade his rebellion. And now, one of my cousin wolves will die in my stead, for my sin."

"Andreas, even if you could have stopped Stephen, what he does now he does of his own free will. You *cannot* hold yourself responsible for this."

The king of wolves stared into the distance. "I don't even understand. My brother may be rebellious and proud, but he is not a killer. He is not a—"

His words stopped suddenly.

"Andreas?" Bearing her axes in her grip, Gerwalta turned back to him. "He is not a *what?*"

Suddenly, her companion shook his head, as though waking from a reverie. "It does not matter. I will take the wolf, Gerwalta, for it is my sins for which he bleeds. I will not put this on you. I will not condemn you in my people's eyes in that way."

"Your people would think less of me for killing a natural wolf?"

She left unspoken the obvious question: why should the king wolf care so much why his packlings thought of her anyway?

He nodded.

"Why? They are beasts, not rational creatures."

"The lupines say the same thing of you."

Without deference to her modesty, the konigswolf shifted then, and dashed off in the direction of the pack racing towards its doom.

The pack of seven moved along a stream. Compared to a lupine, the natural wolf looked tiny. Barely the size of Maximillian's hounds, the creatures would come up only to a hand above her knee if they stood beside Gerwalta. What they lacked in height, however, was accommodated by sheer mass. Even through the fur, their muscles rippled, with haunches as thick as tree trunks.

Unlike lupines, the pack moved with an odd sense of

connectedness, as though they were different fingers of a hand reaching in the same direction instead of individual creatures. Two wolves at the center stood out by virtue of the deference the rest of the pack gave them. *The king and queen,* Gerwalta concluded, *or at least, whatever way they are known by the rest of the pack.* They would not be her target, for the effect that would render on the pack as a whole did not serve her purpose. Instead, her eyes focused on the smallest of the wolves, a brawny-colored male with yellow eyes and a ripped ear.

She looked at the base of the tree she'd climbed, catching Andreas's green eyes. Eyes that stayed human despite the canine features that surrounded them. Her finger sliced the air, pointing to the intended target. Andreas looked to the pack, observed for a moment, then hunched down. The patches of brown and flaxen fur blended against the forest floor, like patches of sunlight dappling the earth. His movements defined stealth, each step calculated and placed in such a way as to cause no sound. Even as Andreas approached, a gentle breeze blowing his scent away, the pack remained unaware.

Until Gerwalta herself, vying for a better view, leaped one tree closer. The act itself did not rouse them to her presence, but her losing her grip on her ax handle did.

*Phhwehhh... flmp.*

The pack lifted their collective heads form the stream, one of them yipped, and they were off.

"Damn it!"

The wolfsretter fell. No time for grace, she must keep up. Andreas had a head start, and it was his tail, not theirs, she tagged to follow. Her cloak flew out behind her as feet pelted ground, buying up the distance between them. Soon, she found herself beside Andreas's hindquarters, then his maw, and a moment later, she had surpassed him.

*"Woohlph!"*

If he thought she'd understand, he was mistaken. As it was, there was no time to stop and wonder what he was trying to say. The wolves were in sight, just a little ahead. The smallest one took up the rear, and ahead of him, three... no, four more.

Which left three unaccounted for. Had they split off?

It was a question she would not have to engage much though in, for in the next step she took, it was upon her.

It had to be the king wolf. None other of the pack were this size.

*It will go for your throat.* The lessons of her training resurfaced in a heartbeat. She curled inward, trying to reposition herself completely underneath the beast – not a place she particularly wanted to be, but then again, the underside of a wolf didn't have teeth. Only, able to look up now, she realized the animal atop her was not one of the natural wolves at all. It was Andreas.

The pack wasted no time in surrounding them, the missing three completing a circle. Gerwalta took to her feet, preparing herself for the moment the first would strike.

"Damn lupine!" she bellowed, keeping her eyes busy surveying the pack. "What in the hell were you thinking? Was this all a trick to get me out here to kill me?"

She wished he would shift back into his layform, if for no other reason than having the satisfaction of yelling at and with him, but he stayed in fur. If he heard her words, he gave no indication, instead keeping up the rumble in his chest. The natural wolves began to circle, slow deliberate paces, Andreas turning in time with them, his teeth always bared in the king wolf's direction.

She would get dizzy if this kept up, and while that in itself wasn't a threat, a wolfsretter unable to keep on her own two feet did not live long in battle.

"Enough of this!" she bellowed. "Forward!"

But the moment she lifted her foot, she was pulled back. She looked down to find Andreas's hand, his laymen hand, on her wrist.

"We cannot do this!" His voice approximated the growl of his wolf. "They have done nothing wrong."

Were they just going to pretend they weren't surrounded by wild animals baring white, gleaming fangs. "You came to help me! Don't turn on me now."

"It's not about them. It's about us. I won't let you take one of them, Gerwalta. Hasn't enough innocence been destroyed?"

"Yes, and I will not allow for more." She jerked her hand back. "A boy is dead, and we owe the aggrieved a life. A wolf's blood must soak the ground, and I refuse to let it be yours, Andreas."

She turned, summoning the little bit of silver left concealed on her person. A moment later, a silver knife no longer than her finger appeared in her hand. She pulled it back, aiming for the ripped-eared wolf.

"Gerwalta, no!"

And let it fly.

The victim yelped. The pack scattered. The blade was too small to kill the wolf, but it landed in his chest front leg such that running would not be possible.

Gerwalta seized the moment, pulling the wolf's feet from beneath him before flipping him over on his back and setting about binding his feet with a bit of wire kept always in her pocket.

"Gerwalta, they're going to kill him."

She closed her eyes, lecturing her heart not to reveal the turmoil within. "I know, and I'm sorry, but there's nothing else we can do. I wish there were. I wish I could change..."

She cut herself off before apostasy beset her.

"This is just the way things are."

# SEVENTEEN

He wasn't sure what was the greatest tragedy he could attribute to this day, when there were so many from which to choose. Was it that he'd confirmed his brother had killed an innocent child and attempted to frame Andreas himself for the murder? Or perhaps the fact that another lupine from outside his pack had been involved, bringing an unknown third party into what should have only been family business?

Could he point to the fact that, having caught an innocent natural wolf to serve judgment for Stephen's heinous actions, it was Andreas himself who, forced by the need to keep their cover, carried the creature's bound body back to the village? That would have been a grievous deed, but none of these things weighed as heavily on him as the most transformative event this day... Lo, any of his days.

For one brief moment, he'd wanted the wolfsretter as his mate.

The howls of a hundred generations of his forebears couldn't recall the desire that welled up within him hearing her simple plea: *kiss me.* Andreas tried to rationalize his longing. Lupines had been bullied and coerced by their kind for centuries; how could he not feel a rush of vengeance overtake him when the auburn-haired and ivory-skinned Gerwalta Faust presented a golden opportunity to take advantage of her innocence? Or was it *she* who took advantage of *him*? Surely Fraulein Faust would know his loyalties would be tested by uncovering Stephen's misdeeds. Did she believe he could be swayed by the promise of her affections? It would be just like her type, to use a lupine's reliance on physical sensation for the base of action.

But the moment he'd watched her tackle the wolf he now bore on his shoulders, tying its limbs together the way he tied a calf or a pig to take it to market...

The forlorn faces of the somber village hunting party blinked and brightened when they came into sight, driving deeper his guilt. Before he could spoil their festivities, Gerwalta rounded on them and dappled lies with the ease of a child blowing on a frosted dandelion.

Artifice came so naturally for her. He'd have to remember that.

"Bernhard! Oh, Bernhard, you won't believe it! Andreas here was very sad he couldn't assist you, and he got the notion in his head that he was just as capable of hunting as you all were. Well, I tried to talk him out of it, but you know how he gets. He ran off into the forest, and nary a weapon on him at all! By the time I tracked him down, there he was, holding the wolf and stroking it like he was holding a puppy! Luckily, I'd managed to take of a spool of wire I saw in that barn we stayed in last night, so we were able to bind the wolf and bring him here. Isn't that marvelous?"

But in her eagerness to cover their truth, Gerwalta's lies had been spread too thin. A man wearing a sneer and incredulity in his features stepped forward.

"Spool of wire from the barn, you say?"

Gerwalta flinched for only a moment. "Yes, I hope that was all right."

The poor girl, rarely found outside her family's luxurious castle and who had probably never been in a barn before the previous night, couldn't have known how precious such a commodity was. That a village farmer without a noble patron would have little if any wire, let alone a spool of it, could never have occurred to her. She just assumed.

Luckily, Bernhard Dreger picked up on his kin's misfortune. He rushed forward, rubbing her arm as though petting a dog. "That is great news, dear, but I'm afraid that was *our* wire. I took it from our cart last night to keep it from rusting in the rain or being stolen."

Right on cue, Gerwalta manufactured a pout. "Oh, dear... I didn't know, darling. Well, in any case, we *can* remove it once we return the cursed creature to the pit, could we not? It will still be usable?"

He took her tiny, dangerous hands in his. "Of course." Then turning to Andreas, Bernhard kept up the act. "Well, then, Andreas, what are you waiting for? Put it in the well. It's just over there."

Andreas sighed and shut his eyes. Every tear-stained mourner's eye in the proximity fell upon him, and the weight of their expectations almost buried him. As though reminding Andreas that they were not so different, the wolf atop his shoulders whined. Cried. Called on a brethren for mercy. The konigswolf commanded his feet to move, but his body protested what his soul knew to be wrong.

His eyes flew open when Gerwalta's arm hooked his, and began to pull him and the wolf toward their ruin. "What are you doing? Walk!" she whispered so silently only a dark one would be able to hear her.

Andreas shook his head. "His blood... His blood will be on my hands."

"His blood is on Stephen's hands. As is the child's." Then, leaning up, her tones turned acidic. "You or the natural wolf, Herr Baron. One of you will be at the bottom of the well when we leave this village."

He swallowed hard and wondered how he ever could have put his mouth on such a vile creature.

But in the end, she was right. *Lord, as you commanded Abraham, so now Gerwalta Faust commands me. Put in my arms a lamb in the place of this sacrifice, if thou art merciful.*

God may grant grace, but men knew no such beauty. They killed the wolf. They hacked off its maw. They dressed him in clothes and placed a wig atop his head and cursed out his name.

And, yes, Andreas did believe that in the end, that creature looked somewhat like him.

# CHAPTER EIGHTEEN

Stephen had learned to cover his tracks. Or more precisely, how not to leave any.

The female wolf who was traveling with him wasn't as careful. Which meant, either she was foolish, or she was arrogant.

Two days had passed since the village, and other than the occasional utterings necessary when people traveled together, the lupine and the wolfsretter kept their own counsel. Not that Andreas would have been able to get a word in edgewise had he wished to speak; Bernhard's attempts to woo Gerwalta would have been visible to a blind man. It was a curious thing to observe, given how the decision on Gerwalta's husband would be dictated by the Matron. Why was Herr Dreger so fastidious in his campaign for her heart, if the object of his amour did not hold the reigns of her marital fate?

And why was Gerwalta falling for it, knowing that her mother with a snap of her fingers could choose another, rending the daughter's heart in two?

Bernhard insisted that Gerwalta ride in the empty cart as he rode the horse. The male wolfsretter made convincing excuses; even though they arrived in the Bavarian forest, they were still apt to meet laity on the path. A lady would not walk; she'd be given use of any form of comfort they had.

*He dwells too much on the customs of men,* Andreas thought, seeing in retrospect the error of his own abuses against Gerwalta's nature. The woman was a warrior, proud and true, even if green in her practice. It had not been right for him to force her to obey his decree, as though she were one of his packlings. Not that he subscribed to wolfsretter's being superior, but that did not mean he could not give her respect.

How was it that a lupine could understand this, and Dreger, one of her own kind, could not?

Nico and Hans, Herr Dreger's two hired hometown goons,

also rode mount, two mares presented to Andreas as thanks for finding the wolf. They were amazed at his willingness to give up such gifts, but what use did a lupine have for a horse? Unlike cows, sheep, and pigs, the animals were too sensitive to his nature to allow him to mount.

When at last they had some cover of trees, Andreas took his wolf and kept pace in parallel with the others, still traveling by day and stopping at night to maintain the fallacy of their mission. On the third night, he sensed her away from the others and found Gerwalta sitting on the lowest branch of a tree, contemplating the stars.

When their eyes met and Gerwalta conjured her red cloak from nowhere, he thought it may be a sign to keep his distance. When the wolfsretter pulled the garment from her shoulders and tossed it his way, however, he understood her intentions for his modesty.

He suffered through the passing pain, moving from four legs to two in a matter of seconds. Andreas felt like a baby, swaddling himself in her garment, but it was obvious she had something to say to him, being here beyond the earshot of their traveling companions, staring at a moon which grew more pregnant with each night of the journey, swelling his anxiety about the inevitable.

Wolf though he was, Andreas was still a man, and knew to let her come to her words at her own pace.

"I owe you an apology."

"Oh? I didn't know your kind did that."

Gerwalta took the jab in stride, which gave Andreas his second surprise in as many minutes. He ought to just listen to her without rebuke, for how often were occasions when a wolfsretter would lower herself to humility?

Luckily, she picked back up without prompting. "A lupine and a natural wolf are two very different creatures, but you must have felt conflicted nonetheless. I should not have made you do that. It needed to be done, but I should not have made you be the one to bear it to its death. Especially when..." A long inhale, followed by a longer exhale. "Especially when it was my fault that the boy died."

He blinked his confusion. "Fraulein Faust—"

"*Gerwalta*, Andreas." Her bright eyes, their natural blue instead of the inhuman silver they became whenever her pulse picked up, glistened in the moonlight. "I thought we agreed we could allow each other that privilege in private."

"Very well, then, *Gerwalta*." He pulled the cloak around him more tightly and settled next to her on the low-lying branch. "There is some truth to what you say. I am a wolf, and as a wolf, I would want nothing more than to blame a *wolfsretter* for every evil conceivable. But I'm also a man, one who aims to be forthright and moral, and I can in all good conscious assure you that you are not to blame in any fashion for the tragic events in Ansbach. I scented Stephen all over that boy's body."

"But if I had taken Stephen prisoner when we encountered him before..."

"Stop." He put a finger to her mouth, stilling her words. "Do not tread down the path of undone deeds, for it is a never-ending road of fallacy and self-destruction." He dropped his hand just in time to reposition the cloak before it fell to the ground. "What if I had never quarreled with him about wanting to mate a member of the laity? What if I had run just a little faster, no matter how weary I was, and managed to catch him after we separated? What if I had never tried to appeal to him when I got to Ansbach and just fought him there and then?"

"What?" Gerwalta's gaze swung from the sky above to the wolf beside her. "You said you saw him, but you actually *spoke* to him?"

He hadn't meant to keep it secret, though he likewise had not been eager to share. Still questioned why he had. Was it an inclination to slight a wolfsretter, or the guilt at letting the opportunity to stop his brother go to waste? "Yes, briefly. I begged him to give up this foolishness and return with me, but it seems there are bigger games afoot than some eloping lovers."

"Meaning?"

"My brother is planning to reveal our kind to the Emperor, to offer us as soldiers in his armies."

Was it the arch of silver light across the sky above, or the words that made Gerwalta look so pale? "We exist in parallel. Wolfsretter will fall under the royal eye and the holy see as well. It will be the tale of Jataka all over again."

"Jataka?"

She nodded. "A wolfsretter in the House of Amber, long ago

in the distant east. One day the lay prince of her land discovered her in the midst of a hunt. He saw her wield silver. To keep her silence, he demanded she provide him an egg made of silver as a wedding gift, when he wed. She agreed, thinking it a small cost to keep her secret. But the prince tricked her, and married a new girl picked randomly from the villagers each day. Soon, the prince had many silver eggs, but he always wanted more. He thought Jakata *made* the silver, wouldn't believe she could only *reshape* the metal. In anger, he killed her and cut her into pieces, thinking he could find the silver she hoarded inside her. He found nothing, of course."

"It sounds like a nursery story."

"It may be," she conceded. "But that doesn't make it any less possible, or detract from the lesson it teaches. If laymen know of our abilities, they will exploit it until we have nothing more to give. And then they will have our blood. The wolfsretter will perish."

Part of him wanted to say it was about time her kind had a fear of domination by others; lupines certainly had suffered oppression long enough. But some curious quirk in him fretted when he thought of Gerwalta subjugated to the human qualms of god and country. As little sense as that made, it hardly mattered now. There were bigger threats at hand.

"Gerwalta, as much as it pains me to say this, I understand what must be done. I left the Schwarzwald hoping to bring Stephen home, but now my mission must be to stop him at any price. I take some comfort that we have been brought back together, for while I am konigswolf, my palace is a forest, and my subjects, lupines. The castles and court of the laity are something of which I know little, but in which you, reared in matters of diplomacy by your mother, are well versed. If I can get close to Stephen, I will ensure he either submits, or yields. But I cannot do this alone."

He reached for her by instinct, but delighted when she did not pull away. Her hand... It was so lithe, so soft, so velvety. How could this be the hand of so demonstrable a foe? How could so tiny a hand, which fit so naturally into his, be of a creature born to tyrannize his pack?

"Gerwalta, please. Help me do this. Not for me, but for all wolves and—"

"It was my mother's wish that I allow Stephen to get to court."

Shock blew back his touch. "What?"

"She…" Internal strife played across her features. "The Matron saw an opportunity to allow me to spy at court. She commanded that I allow Stephen to flee long enough so that I could have an excuse to visit."

"But why would…" Reasons permeated his thoughts and searched for words, but found them lacking. "What cause would Frau Faust have in that?"

"My family has been the supplier of silver and craftsman of its implementation to the imperial court for a century, but recently, they've turned favor from us. It is hurting my mother's purse."

He sucked on his bottom lip. "Your lot commands silver. How could you possibly be hurting in the purse?"

"Not all debts can be paid in silver, Herr Baron. We require the same things you do: foodstuffs, linens, taxes. Silver pays taxes and buys influence, but it is not accepted by a cheesemaker or a carpenter without talk. And as Jakata's prince learned, we do not *create* it. Its supply is not inexhaustive, for if was, it would not have nearly as much value as it does."

He nodded as the truth sunk further down. "So your mother was using my brother's betrayal to her advantage? How dare she… How dare any of you—"

Before Andreas understood what was happening, his words died as Gerwalta threw her arms around him and buried her head into his chest.

"I never would have agreed." Hot tears fell down her face and soaked the downy, sparse fur that followed him into a layman. "If I thought it was going to mean an innocent boy would die, and that I'd have to force you to sacrifice a natural wolf for my oversight, and that you'd have to hunt and kill your own kin, I never… But to think it almost led to your death… Andreas, I… I…"

"Shh…" Her auburn hair, laced in braids that ran down her back, still managed to be soft under his palm despite its binding. "Hush, now. I never would have sought her help if I had thought it would lead to you and me—"

Big blue eyes found him in the darkness when she looked up, and it didn't take long for her lips to follow.

On the occasion of their previous kiss, Andreas had complied to her request more as a dare than a desire. This time, when his mouth began to move against hers and his hands rose to thread through her hair, pushing lose her auburn braids, it was for no other reason than he wanted to partake of her.

Because *he* wanted *her.*

Gerwalta moaned into his mouth, the tiniest vibration that sent his animal urges soaring. He couldn't remember when he'd let go of the red cloak that hid his modesty, or when the two of them had moved from sitting on the branch to lying on the ground, her body beneath his and her thighs pressing into his hips, holding him in place.

He pulled back only when breathing demanded it. Gerwalta's eyes shone in the darkness, two gleaming silver discs which blinked into existence when she realized he'd stopped.

"Why are you doing this?" he demanded. Only, was he asking her, or himself?

"I shouldn't. It's forbidden. If my mother ever discovered I'd kissed you... There is no greater crime for a wolfsretter than to give herself to a wolf."

"Crime?" Andreas pushed himself up on his arms, hovering over her. "What is the punishment?"

"Death for the wolf, exile for the wolfsretter." She blinked up at him. "Is this not forbidden for lupines?"

"Of course not, though I can't imagine a konigswolf would take well one of his packlings mating a wolfsretter. Death seems a bit of an overreaction, though." He lowered himself again, pulling towards her lips. "But it may be worth it."

And as though she'd awoken from a dream, Gerwalta lashed her eyes closed and began to slide out from under him.

"The moon!" She grumbled as she rose to his feet, pointing skyward and laying all blame on the celestial bodies overhead. "We're two nights from the full moon, and it's... *doing* things to us."

Andreas doubted it. Otherwise, the scenes that would ensue each month between lupines and patrolling wolfsretter of the Schwarzwald would make a cow blush. Nonetheless, Gerwalta had been right to note the precarious tilt of the lunar cycle. In two nights, Stephen would fall victim to the moon's pull, powerless to stop the shift. If he were in the hands of the laity when that happened, what would become of him?

And what would that mean for them all?

Andreas was pulled from his reverie by Gerwalta's perturbed voice. "I am so sorry, Herr Baron. I am young, and unwed, and I... I..."

"You desire a man in your bed."

His bold assertion turned her apologies to shock. "You must think me wicked for thinking of such low acts in times such as these."

"It is never wicked to want what is natural." He couldn't help the errant thoughts running like rabbits through a meadow in the garden of his mind. "You do have... options, Gerwalta." His eyes turned meaningfully back to the direction of the fire where the others lay fast asleep as he too gathered his feet beneath him. "Bernhard seems quite taken with you, and you do not shun his attention. Your kind does not have the lifelong consequences we wolves do from... such informal dalliances."

She crossed one arm over her stomach to grab the opposite elbow, rubbing the back of her neck with her free hand. "There are other consequences than a mating bond to consider. And there's...."

Her eyes burned even brighter, if it was possible. Wide gazed and looking like she'd been struck by lightning, Gerwalta turned to him. "Was it only one wolf who killed the boy?"

Andreas felt sweat dapple his brow, heard his own heartbeat pounding in his ears. His mouth dried. His pulse spiked. "How did you know that?"

The wolfsretter's mouth transformed into a scowl. "All the reports of livestock attacks... Both Bernhard and I being sent at the same time to chase down rogue wolves... The imperial court shifting its silver supplies from our stocks..."

She reached for him, pulling Andreas by the hand, deeper into the forest. "Your brother is walking into a trap."

"What?" With a forceful tug, he managed to both stop their forward advance and spin Gerwalta his direction. "Gerwalta, what are you talking about? How did you know about the second wolf? What does it have to do with anything?"

"Don't you think it funny, Andreas? We set out from Triberg at almost the same time Bernhard is sent by his mother, one of the vicematrons under my mother's command, from Ravensburg, both of us pursuing a lone wolf? When he said he was following the report of a wolf, those may have been his mother's words. I assumed it was Stephen, but no, there *is* a second wolf, one I am willing to bet defected from the Ravensburg pack, lured away by some lady love to the imperial court. And probably, far more than that, all coming together on a full moon. Think about it, Andreas. Your brother told you this woman and he were going to reveal lupines to the king, did he not?"

"Yes, but…"

"Stephen is your brother, and I do not doubt he is such a different man than you are. He would not leave his pack to be with some laywomen, knowing that he'd go mad in a few months. I know the saying goes love drives one to madness, but I do not think one preempts the journey for the sake of love."

He could argue strongly with her on that. Another time, perhaps. For the moment, the outlines of what the wolfsretter was presenting began to take shape in his understanding. "Someone's creating a new pack, a feat that takes a female and male wolf. That's why the other wolf I detected in Ansbach was a woman."

She looked into the distance. "You can learn that from the scent left on a victim?"

"Of course." He bit his tongue before telling her how he could smell something very female and very enticing about her even at this moment. "I'm sorry I didn't tell you, but the other wolf is not my pack. She is not my problem to solve."

Gerwalta's hand tightened into a fist. "No, but she's mine. Someone's trying to form a pack loyal to the crown. Your brother has been hoodwinked. Come, we must make it to Nuremberg by full moon."

"Wait!" He arrested her hand and pulled her back around. "What about Herr Dreger?"

"You mean my well-intentioned cousin who keeps insisting that I, a woeful woman, should not do my duty merely because I am the fairer sex?" Gerwalta rolled her eyes. "Do not misconstrue my meaning. Bernhard is a righteous wolfsretter and a brave warrior, but I've grown weary of his attempts to preserve my honor by locking me away."

He swelled with pride at hearing her put the boorish brute in his rightful place. "Then we depart without him. Though I must point out, it will be difficult for me to get into the imperial court without clothing."

Her eyes cast down as her cheeks reddened, as though Gerwalta had just remembered that a nude man stood before her. Or perhaps recalling that same said nude man had been atop her and kissing her breathless just a few moments before.

"Not to mention, all our provisions are with the others," he continued. "We'll be trying to accomplish two days of travel in half that time, all without any funds or food."

"Surely between the two of us we can make do with what the forest and our wits provide."

"And do you have silver enough to purchase appropriate attire for me when we get to the city?"

"I hope so." Her hand when to her chest, rubbing her rib cage. "Though I will owe apologies to all the gentlewomen of Nuremberg for denying them the view."

All the breath escaped him, but before he could say anything to follow, Gerwalta retrieved her cloak and took to the trees.

He took to his fur and followed.

# NINETEEN

Gerwalta ran.

Not for the sake of reaching Nuremberg, though that was, of course, the goal. She ran forward, ever forward, because if she paused for a moment, she'd have to face Andreas, and the truth of what had happened – *was happening* – between them.

Though, she promised herself, nothing *further* would happen. Not so much had transpired, if she thought about it. She'd merely kissed Andreas. Twice. And pulled him atop of her, but that, only once. If anyone found out, could she merely claim that she'd been teasing the wolf, playing into his fantasies to earn his cooperation and get her to court? It would be believable, as long as nothing further happened between them.

And it wouldn't. It *couldn't.*

She paused on a branch, pushing her fingers to her lips and whistling. The wolf on the forest floor beneath her bayed before coming into sight. In two clicks, he grew into a man.

"What is it?"

Gerwalta pointed to the horizon, to where a hill rose in the distance, veins of stone streets, timbered houses, and the tower of a castle on its highest peak. A bright red banner flapped against the pale blue sky.

"The emperor is in residence."

Andreas's hand went to his brow as he squinted, the sun framed just over her shoulder. Already at midday, the beams of light served as a clock ticking down the hours until sunset. "If you're close enough to see the flag, you're close enough to be seen by them. Come out of the trees."

He had a good point. Probably best to do away with the red cloak as well. In a sigh, its existence ceased. Gerwalta stepped off the branch and proceeded to fall at a very slow, and very leisurely, speed.

By the time she'd come to ground, Andreas's jaw had come to rest atop the leaves as well. "You can fly."

"No, I cannot."

"Well, you certainly didn't *fall* out of the tree. I could have run to the river and back in the time you took to reach the ground."

"It's rude to criticize." Gerwalta fished out the clothing she'd bought off a peddler on the side of the road earlier that morning. They'd be too loose below and too tight above, but Andreas would be clothed. "Only Matrons fly. It's considered a divine sign of one's propensity towards leadership. Now, put these on. We should be to the city walls in an hour or two, and we'll purchase you something better fitted there. Speaking of the river, I'm going to go refill our skins. We'll head back to the road and—"

He grabbed her hand and twirled her as she attempted to walk away. "I bet that's how you jump so high, so easily, isn't it?"

"*All* wolfsretter can jump high."

"Not like you. You were up in the top of that barn in Ansbach. That had to be the height of three men, and there wasn't a ladder anywhere! And why you jumped into that pit without fear of how you would get out." He let go her hand and twirled. "It was amazing. *You're* amazing. Just when I think I've come to understand you, you have another secret. But, wait." His words died in the air along with any trace of joy in her features. "If it is considered a sign of one meant to be Matron, does that mean you—"

"It means nothing," she interjected. "It is ancient foolishness, old superstitions."

Understanding failed him. "But to lead a pack—a *clan,* is a great honor. Why would you not want that?"

"Because the last thing I want to be like is my mother," she said stoically. "Severe, withdrawn, always keeping my children at a distance and only seeing them as pawns in securing my power. I *want* to be married off, Andreas. Perhaps it will mean leaving the Schwartzwald and rearing young in one of our lesser territories, but it will remove me from that horrid home where I am always another thread for others to spin."

"But as Matron, you'd have the ability to change all that," he argued.

"No, Helga will be Matron," she insisted. "It has been expected since we were young. This last fortnight, seeing the torment you're going through having to oppose your own sibling, makes me realize how much I'd never want to be on the other side of mine."

Gerwalta shook her head, and shooed away the subject. "We don't have time to dwell on this. We must press on. Come, we're running out of time."

Two things could kill a wolf: silver inside the head, or silver to the heart. Gerwalta was his silver, and she was burning a hole both above and below.

It was foolish to let himself fall for the wolfsretter. No good could come of it. They'd never be together, they certainly *could* never be together. Oh, he was fairly certain he could seduce her, if that's all he was after. Some part of him took devious glee at the prospect of ruining one of her kind for all others. But it would ruin him too, for to lay with Gerwalta would trigger his mating bond. His heart would forever be hers, and no doubt she'd stomp on it. Away from Schloss Wolfsretter, on her life's first grand adventure, she'd indulge a thrill, embraced him in passing. But as soon as she saw how he'd grovel at her feet once bonded, she'd lose all respect for him. Her heart would have no such restrictions, and how would he cope when she inevitably moved on to another?

They arrived at the city walls as the sun turned down from its zenith. A crowd milled about, waiting to pass through the gates into the safety of the city before nightfall. Andreas tried to arrest the overdrive of his senses. Villages were taxing enough, but this... There were too many scents, too many noises, too much to see. The konigswolf closed his eyes, breathed in, tasted the air. Bread, meats, rot, urine, flowers, mud, perfume... It all swirled together in a miasma of experiences not his own. He felt dizzy, overwhelmed, clingy. He reached for Gerwalta's hand as his body swayed.

"I know." Her body became the foundation which lifted him. "It's hard for me, too."

"People. Everywhere." He leaned on her. "So many people."

"It will be easier once we're inside the palace walls," she assured him. "Come."

A ripping of cloth hit his ears, followed a moment later by pressure against his eyes.

"My father does this with the horses when he fears there's too much to worry them. I know you're not a horse, but perhaps it will help."

"It does." And it did. Simplistic though it was, it did. "Thank you."

She pulled him like the blind man he'd become through the gates and streets of Nuremberg. "My medallion bears my family crest. It should get us into the castle if I claim to be representing my father on business to the court."

"Don't you mean your mother?"

"No, we're in the heart of the lay world now. My mother, as a woman, has little standing here. It is my father, or sometimes my brother, who must always conduct our business with men."

Foolish laity. Unlike the matriarchal wolfsretter, wolves were always ruled by a male member of the pack, but a king wolf would never dare insinuate his mate was his inferior or not due respect and deference merely because she was female. "Are either your father or your brother known at the imperial court?"

"No. All our affairs are conducted through the Duke of Württemberg or by correspondence."

Andreas turned, forcing Gerwalta to the end of his arms. He took off the cloth covering his eyes and pulled at the leather cord which hung around her neck. "I'll have to pretend to be your brother, then. I'm far too young to stand place for your father. His name is Maximilian, is it not?"

"Andreas!" She clasped his hands. "Don't be foolish. If the silver touches your skin..."

"Then I'll be careful it doesn't," he insisted, very delicately pulling it off her neck. "If a woman from a wealthy family comes seeking business without a proper letter of introduction or chaperone, it could raise suspicions. We must be quick. Sunset is hours away. I feel its weight in my soul."

And as he delicately leaned forward and slipped the cord around his neck, he felt the weight of the silver as well. It settled on his chest, two layers of clothing the only thing keeping it from burning another scar into his flesh. Andreas delicately teased the metal disc under his jacket but above his undershirt, feeling like a man as he was being shoved into to a torture chamber, moments before the door closed. The object of his death was so close, it had merely to move into place to kill him.

Luckily, the wolfsretter protested no more. There was logic in his actions, and she knew it. "Can you sense Stephen? Would you be able to sense the other wolf?"

He shook his head. "I'd be able to smell her if I crossed her trail, but I can't perceive wolves not of my pack like that. What about you? I thought wolfsretter could sense any wolf if they were close enough."

She closed her eyes, breathed deep, exhaled.

When she kept silence, he prodded her. "What is it? Do you sense them? Which direction?"

"Every direction. I…"

But she never got to finish what she was saying, for a moment later, Andreas felt the sword at his back and his hands went into the air.

# TWENTY

In a heartbeat, Gerwalta overrode the anxiety of her senses and assessed the surroundings.

An imperial guard, distinctive by his red and black stripped pantaloons, held a weapon to Andreas's back which she couldn't see. Short sword? Perhaps, but from the angle of his shoulder, more than likely a dagger. The guard behind him, however, had three blades within command, including the one whose hilt was in hand. They'd angled themselves away from the street where common folk went about their business. They didn't want to bring attention, but why not could be anyone's guess.

"Fraulein." It had been so long since Andreas had addressed her formally, it sounded foreign from his lips. "I'm sure these guards only wish to detain us and bring us inside for further questioning by their superiors. No need for dramatics."

"This smithy speaks true." The larger of the two guards jerked his head toward the gateway. "Make no fuss, and we'll make no holes into you."

Heart racing, she somehow managed to calm her nerves, ease her hands, relax her posture. "Very well. Gentlemen, please…"

Nuremberg Castle, one of the jewels of the Holy Roman Emperor's crown, didn't impress her nearly as much as she'd supposed it would. Perhaps because she'd been raised in a castle, if one much smaller. Its luxuries didn't surpass Schloss Wolfsretter; there were merely more of them for the eye to behold. Its walls would be easily scaled by a dark one, and to her quick observation, only its central tower which she'd observed even from far outside the city, appeared to be truly secure.

Immediately past the first bailey, the guards took them left, then right, and then they began to descend a winding stairway, all the while the tingle in Gerwalta's fingers growing stronger. That she had more silver to craft a weapon like her hand ached to hold! She dare not speak; just because the guards had obviously known they were wanted didn't mean they knew why, nor what they were.

When they entered a corridor lit dimly by torches, Andreas's hand found hers, clutching so tightly he threatened to drive all the blood from her fingers. A moment later, she knew why.

Their scent saturated the senses.

"Go to the end of the hall, then knock once," the guard said, giving them both a push forward. "We'll be here just long enough to make sure you don't turn and run."

Andreas hissed, and Gerwalta suddenly remembered the injury caused when he saved her from the lightning. It would heal with the passing of a full moon, he'd said, but that event had not yet had a chance to pass.

"Do you scent Stephen on the air?"

The konigswolf stopped, taking in a long draw of air through his nose, closing his eyes in concentration. A moment later, they opened again, reading of sadness. "No."

Gerwalta paced on. "No matter, we must see this through."

"Gerwalta, wait." He pulled her back. "I should go first. They will expect that."

"Wouldn't lupines be more cordial to a lupine leading a wolfsretter?"

"Or find it suspicious. But then again, I am supposed to be a *male* wolfsretter, so would I lead a *female* wolf?"

"Of course, you would! You'd lead *any* wolf, because as a wolfsretter, *any* wolf is your inferior and beneath you."

"So you're saying you should be beneath me? Mayhap being a wolfsretter is not so bad."

"Are you sincerely making a jest at a time like this?"

Having reached the door, and with the guards still poised at the far end of the hall, Andreas made to raise a balled fist. Gerwalta managed to knock it away just as he tapped. She tried then, getting just treatment from him. In the end, neither would know who knocked, but they would both remember they'd entered the room together.

It seemed a veritable children's story, one filled with genies and shahs and silver chalices. How had such a room, in which opulent lounging couches covered in fine oriental fabrics encircled a wooden table atop which a golden plate the size of a shield held the last fruits of summer exist in this castle? More than that, how did its occupants come to be? On every surface, a lupine. A dozen total, each in the distinct dress and manner of his origins. Gerwalta knew something of regional variations of fashion. On occasions when other wolfsretter visited her mother's court, she had learned their manner. That one was Prussian, the red-haired wolf Flemish, and one wore a hat she thought similar to that of a distant cousin from Budapest.

As Andreas had concluded, none proved to be Stephen. The one at the center of all their attention, however, *was* female.

Radiance did not suit to describe her. Tall, shapely, with blonde hair peeking out from under an elaborate headdress of gold and red. The fabric twisted around her waist in a golden and purple thread must be silk. Gerwalta had seen it on each of her sister's bridal gowns, and remembered its reflective sheen. Around the lady's bodice, feathers dyed in colors like those of her red-yellow dress and cape gave her a plumaged appearance.

The woman was a noble, no doubt of that. But given the tingles in Gerwalta's chest when she concentrated on her, she was also a wolf.

She stepped forward, taking the eyes of the dozen wolves seated on sofas and propped up with pillows around the room. "You've come a long way to be here, haven't you?" she said in Andreas's direction. "And to do that and give yourself away at the last minute by flashing your medallion in public, it really was quite..." She rolled her fingers. "Amateur."

Gerwalta instinctively clutched at her chest, her heart leaping. Only then did she recall that it now hung from Andreas's neck. They'd bought the ruse so easily, it almost concerned her. But, if Andreas could only sense his own pack, surely the same was true of other wolves. They could smell wolf, of course, but there were so many other scents from those assembled, not to mention the underlying aroma of mildew that hung in the air, for despite the pretty dressing they were still in a dungeon. It may be too difficult for the female to discern that it was *Andreas* and not *she* who was the wolf.

"I am Aldhild, and I am the queen of this pack." The beautiful shewolf turned on heel to Gerwalta. "What is your name, and how did you come to be here? My invitation was only to *male* wolves."

"Queen?" Andreas asked. "Who is king?"

"There is no king, measly wolfsretter," Aldhild hissed. "Your kind probably thinks you are the only dark creature who can be ruled by a woman, don't you? I cannot blame you; most of my kind thinks the same. The members of my pack, however, have learned better."

A low rumble of laughter came with the queen's flicked finger inviting the reaction. When she turned on Gerwalta, the distraction had allowed sufficient time to conceive a cover story.

"My name is Rohese." Where it had come from, she knew not, but there was no time to hesitate, and no opportunity to offer alternatives. "I followed my cousin, unbeknownst to him, to see where he was going."

"Your cousin?" She looked in turn to each of the wolves on the perimeter. "And which of my strapping beasts is he?"

"I do not see him here," Gerwalta admitted. "His name is Stephen."

"Ah, *him*." The shewolf's eyes brightened with understanding. "Stephen unfortunately failed to prove his worth to me when given the chance."

Beside her, Andreas stiffened.

But Gerwalta had dealt with enough powerful women to know the truth usually remained in the shadow of the spoken. "Do you mean killing the child outside Ansbach?"

Aldhild nodded. "There's no place in my pack for a wolf who refuses *any* order I issue. Once he refused to kill the boy, I knew he never would be capable of seeing out our vision. Stephen even fought me when I gave him a second chance, telling him to stand aside as *I* killed the boy. Me! He even tried to save him. But Ansbach was some time ago, and I left Stephen in no condition to follow me. How is it, then, that you were still able to track us all the way here to Nuremberg?"

Gerwalta laced her hands behind her back. "When I could not find Stephen's trail out of the village, I picked up yours."

From the corner of her eye, she saw Andreas flinch. Something about that wouldn't add up.

"I am very careful not to leave a trail," Aldhild insisted, suspicion narrowing her gaze.

"True, *you* did not," Gerwalta admitted. "And most wolves—pardon, most *male* wolves," she let the dispersion settle around to the affronted parties before continuing, "would have abandoned the quest there. But after the villagers told me about an imperial coach that had passed through town the day before, an auspicious event for someplace as insignificant as Ansbach, I assumed there was a connection. His majesty owns very many fine stallions, but none of them as yet bred without the ability to stink. *Their* trail was all too simple to follow."

Aldhild's arm lashed in Gerwalta's direction. "There, boys!" she said, grinning. "There is why a female is your natural superior. She sees not just the prey, but it's environment. Tell me, Rohese, what news of your cousin? I left him alive. Barely, but still."

Gerwalta hid the smile when she noticed Andreas's frame ease with relief.

"Stephen is no longer my concern." She folded her arms over her chest. "He was always a bit of an embarrassment anyhow."

"And the wolfsretter?" Aldhild asked. "How is it that he came to be in your company?"

To his credit, Andreas did not miss a beat, though his spirit must have been shaking upon learning the news about Stephen. "I am with her because I am a fool," he said. "She manipulated me, seduced me while not whetting my thirst. My heart burns with desire, and she mocks it."

Gerwalta affected her best seductress, turning to Andreas and running a fingertip down his chin, over his chest, tracing his ribs. She didn't know if Andreas was acting or not when his eyes fluttered closed and he took on the expression of the love-drunk.

"Easy, darling. I only said I could not mate you yet, not with the permission of my king. Or perhaps, my queen."

Aldhild blinked. "And you think I would invite you to my pack?"

"I'm saying I would be interested in exploring that

opportunity." She lifted herself to Andreas, praying he wouldn't do anything to give away their lie, and pressed a kiss to his lips. Then, turning a bold brow to Aldhild, added, "It comes with a very obedient wolfsretter who has told me all their secrets. Oh, yes, over the last week or so, Maximillian has been *quite* the songbird. For example—" Gerwalta stepped forward, her hands very suggestively tugging at the brocade cord tied around Aldhild's waist. "Did you know that a wolfsretter is powerless to break a silken restraint?"

The queen's eyebrow arched. "Surely one of us would have known that if it were true."

"Perhaps, but then again—" Gerwalta set about untying the simple knot that kept Aldhild's corded belt from falling, then eased it over her hips, into her hands. "Have you ever seen a wolfsretter *wearing* silk?"

The queen shook her head. "Bind him then, and let us talk more. Frederick!"

At her bellow, one of the larger wolves leaped forward. "Yes, my queen."

"Put Maximillian in a cell. Rohese and I are going to have a little chat, shewolf to shewolf."

# TWENTY-ONE

Frederick, along with a rather dullard of a wolf whose name turned out to be Wilhelm, led Andreas to his "cell" — a side room without windows and with a heavy iron door. Even for a wolf, Andreas struggled to see in through the blanket of black. Luckily, his ears worked fine, and his captors were either too foolish or too confident to observe silence within earshot of where they kept guard.

"Think she'll join us, that Rohese one?"

That from Wilhelm, whose accent suggested German was not his first tongue.

"Hope so," Frederick responded, the lilt in his voice signifying he was very, very Saxon. "If the queen's plan succeeds, we'll need to start mating immediately to grow our pack. Strength in numbers, as they say. And that Rohese… Let's just say it wouldn't disappoint me if she ended up in my sheets."

Andreas fought the urge to use the strength he knew he possessed as a konigswolf to push open the door and force both the insolent curs into submission.

"Yeah, but you heard what that wolfsretter said." Here Andreas could picture the two wolves motioning to the closed door behind them. "'Seduced me.' *Seduced.* You don't think she's already given her bond to *him*, do you?"

Frederick chuckled. "What would ever possess a wolf to turn his back on his kind and mate with the enemy?"

*Love would, you fools. Love would possess him!*

The errant thought flashed through his mind too quickly to recall… and there it was. The truth, undeniable and resilient, that had laid hidden behind a wall of history and tradition his heart had been pulling down, brick by brick, since they'd left Triberg. All Andreas's biases, all his kind's past, all his notions of proper and possible… they surrendered to the immutable reality. He *loved* Gerwalta. He wanted her, as his bride, as his mate, as the mother of his pups.

It was treason.

It was salvation.

It would be the death of him, quite literally, if it ever became known to her clan.

This love was *deadly.*

Bogged down by the enormity of his heart's revelation, Andreas lost track of what the two wolves prattled on about, or how much time passed. Other than the growing pull in his innards, the sensation present whenever full moon was nigh, he became unaware of his physical connection to the world, drifting away on flights of fancy of ways he might be able to woo the wolfsretter.

She slipped into his cell between his vision of her on their wedding day, and his dreams of their wedding night. So distracted was he, that Andreas took a moment to realize the form of his beloved was asking him a question.

"What?"

"Did they hurt you?" she said in a whisper, though with such annoyance in her tone he knew that she must have said it more than once.

"No, I'm…" Andreas clicked his tongue against a dry palate. "You are a brilliant creature, Gerwalta."

"It will all come to naught if you don't listen to me and do exactly as I—"

Wolfsretter may play politics, but wolves wore their hearts on their hides. Now that he knew, she must too. "I love you."

Her suddenly silver eyes blinked bright in the darkness. "Come again?"

Had he not been bound, he would have taken her into his arms and kissed her proper. At least those peculiar glowing orbs of hers gave him an approximate target. Andreas leaned in, pressing his lips to hers, waiting for her to understand his intentions. None came, though the mere fact that he touched her sent a wave of lust, driven by the moon, spiking through him.

The silk cord only tightened as he pulled on his restraint, but his ardor cooled when he felt the sting of silver press against his chest "I said, I love y——"

"I heard what you said! Are you moonmad already? We haven't time for your soggy emotions! We are in terrible peril, and I only have a moment or two to explain to you how we're to survive. I need you to be the konigswolf right now, *not* some confessor of puppy love."

"Do you doubt the virility of my feelings?"

"I do not doubt the virility of your *anything,*" she confessed. "As my mother would say, shove it down! There is work to be done."

"But we must——"

"*Zzst!*" Gerwalta hissed as she pushed the palm of her hand to his mouth and tried to press on as if he hadn't just laid bare his heart to her. "Now, listen. Aldhild has lured away a wolf from each of the packs within a ten-day journey of Nuremberg, each of them the brother of a king. Stephen was just one of those whose allegiance she stole."

"A female lupine running a pack," he grumbled. "Such an unnatural abomination."

"As a woman descended from a long line of female leaders, I'm going to pretend I didn't hear that. Anyhow, she says there is something called *lupus regina* in legend, a female wolf as a sort of empress of kings. She plans to ally herself with the laity crown, royal to royal, as it were."

"I have... heard tell of this," Andreas admitted, schooling his animal mind to ignore how close she remained. "They say the mother of Romulus and Remus was such a creature, but I thought it was always a myth."

"Are *we* not myth, Andreas?" Gerwalta asked. "Aldhild intends to remake our world. She thinks the time has come for the emperor to become the master of the church, not the other way around, and she intends to be the power behind the crown."

"And she told you all this openly, willingly? How is it that she even believes *you* are a wolf?"

"Because I am a woman. And because the pull of the moon has

disabled her rationality as it does with your kind. *And* because I've spent so much time with you, I *smell* like you."

He felt a hedonic pull in his groin at the thought that he'd marked her, but pushed it down. Gerwalta was right; he'd seduce her later, when they were both certain they would survive.

"She has offered me a place in her pack, but as she's done with each of the other wolves, I must prove my loyalty."

"By agreeing to return to the Schwartzwald and killing the king wolf off? Good of you to agree; it will give us the opportunity to escape and think of..."

"No, Andreas. She thinks you're the wolfsretter, remember?" Through the darkness, Andreas heard Gerwalta's movements as her hands wrapped around his body, taking up the slack of the silk cord which still bound him. "And because I was so able to convince them that I have you smitten and eating out of the palm of my hand..."

"As I just told you, I *am* smitten, and I'll eat out of whatever you tell me to."

She continued as though he had not spoken, "She has asked me to bid you create silver manacles, in which I am to be led into to the emperor's presence just before sunset. When I shift into my wolf, and made calm by her command, you are to release my restraints. Then, to demonstrate the might of a lupine, she will order me to kill you."

There was so much wrong with that, he didn't even know where to begin. "This cannot possibly work."

"Why not? You are a konigswolf. You, like Aldhild, can keep your lay form during a full moon, can you not?"

"So the theory goes, though I have never had a cause as yet to attempt it." He shook his head, even though he knew she could not see it. "Regardless, what goes against us is the fact that you will *not* become a wolf. What will Aldhild do when you prove at sunset not to be a lupine?"

"It doesn't matter!" Gerwalta exclaimed. "I will be bound by silver. I carry my weapon before me as I walk. I know Ferdinand by reputation. He does not abide fools. Once Aldhild is shown to be a fraud, he will order her—and by proxy, us—removed."

"And if she herself takes her wolf and attacks?"

"Did you not hear the part where I said I will be going in with *silver directly at my behest?*"

"And so you will, what? Slay a werewolf before the emperor? Without revealing what you really are?" he asked. "If the emperor learns you can wield silver, I think he'll have more interest in your kind than mine."

"I won't let anyone see. I'm good at hiding my weapons."

"And how, then, shall I go about forming silver manacles? I can't even touch the stuff, let alone craft it into restraints."

"We'll... find a way. We must. There's no..." A hiccup in the air betrayed her. "I will not let her exploit wolves like this. It will either end with your kind being forced into military service, or slaughtered at the order of the church. I will save you. I must save you. I—"

Just then, the door behind them swung open. Though the lantern's light was not bright, it pierced a hole into the darkness that had them both squinting. Their interloper turned out to be Frederick, and the way he molested Gerwalta with his eyes threatened to draw Andreas's wolf to the surface.

"Come now, love, and bring your pet," he said. "Sunset is nigh."

# TWENTY-TWO

Two packlings shepherded them across the courtyard, the inner bailey, and then, the climb started. Up, up, and up, ascending the tower they'd seen even while outside the city, until even a dark one had to pause to catch his breath. Near the top, Aldhild stood outside a heavy oaken door.

"Go below and wait for the others," she told her two wolves. "I will escort them from here."

She slipped an iron key from a hidden pocket of her dress. The shewolf extended a welcoming arm as she opened the door. Even with the setting rays of the sun blasting through a westward arrow slit, the room veritably gleamed.

"Take only what you need, Herr Faust. Quickly, though. Time is running out."

It took a moment for Andreas to remember that, under current circumstances, *he* was the wolfsretter. The werewolf wandered into the room and found himself entombed in silver. He managed to tamp down the screaming voice inside of him that told him to run, that this place was dangerous. And it was, though not just for the obvious reason. The truth remained that he had not gained a magical ability to transform the metal in the last hour. Not for the first time, the konigswolf whispered a silent prayer that Gerwalta had a plan to pull off this farce.

"How is it that you, a lupine, have access to the imperial treasury?" For the moment, he would stall. Within reason, for the sun dipped further down with each passing moment. Even if he, as a konigswolf, could maintain his laymen form, he did not expect it to be easy.

Aldhild grinned her condescension, stepping towards him. "I was able to pull thirteen wolves away from their much-beloved brother kings, and you question my ability to twist the whims of a layman?"

*What would a wolfsretter say? What would a wolfsretter say?* "A wolf

127

who can be either man and beast might be a danger to us as well. It would behove me not to at least ask."

"But it would be foolish of you to expect me to answer." Aldhild flicked an oversized serving bowl setting on a table, drawing a ding with a fingernail and making Andreas flinch in fear of her welfare. "Now, claim your silver and let us be on our way."

Andreas threw his hands up into the air. "What do you propose I do, make my way through the castle clutching tea sets and dining platters to my chest?"

"Or you could just take this cache of silver coins, heartstrings." Gerwalta made both wolves turn at once, kicking a bag formed out of suspiciously red cloth. Its contents clinked. "Dozens of coins, conveniently collected into a sack. Even if they do bear Ottoman markings, silver *is* silver."

The shewolf's head cocked to the side, saying "I do not recall seeing that before," as Andreas made the same motion and, his grin delirious, mouthed to Gerwalta, "heartstrings?"

Gerwalta made work of pulling up the bag from the ground. Even with the protection of the cloth sack, Andreas struggled to overcome his trepidation as she handed it to him. Should one coin fall out as he jostled the surprisingly heavy cache up the stairs and managed to sear his flesh, the game would be up.

He made a show of inspecting the contents. "I suppose this will work well enough, assuming we need only *one* set of manacles and chain."

As Aldhild peered into the bag, he chanced a look at Gerwalta, who gave him an acknowledging nod.

"Fine, then, bring it along."

The shewolf led them from the treasure room. Andreas expected them to head back down at that point, but much to his surprise, they started up, until at last, they came to the end of the stairs and, he'd presume, the top of the tower.

Andreas leaned over to Gerwalta as Aldhild passed until a room behind another door. "A wolf would say 'my pet,' or even 'lambkins,' but never heartstrings."

"Forgive my ignorance, *Herr Faust,* but I am not well acquainted in the language of lovers – lupine or otherwise."

"You will be. Once I've managed to convince you to love me, you'll be able to write poems and compose melodies in thirteen tongues."

Gerwalta strained to keep her voice at a whisper, though the flush in her cheeks was speaking volumes of truth. "Andreas, this is *not* the time for love-making!"

"I agree. Reluctantly." When it was, they would be alone. And undisturbed. And needing provisions for several days. "How were you able to make your cloak into a small sack like this? Can you alter its shape the way you do silver?"

"I didn't alter anything." Her face screwed up. "It was sitting there, with all the coins already in it. Seemed the quickest solution to our query."

"Yes, but what gets us out of the next challenge?" He swallowed down the crawl of his skin, the ache of his bones, forcing his body under his command. "What is taking her so long? Sunset is minutes away."

"We feel it too, you know." Gerwalta turned big blue eyes up to him. "The sunset. It's tugging at my senses."

"Good, then you'll know when to howl. A wolf always does when pulled by the light of the moon. It hurts more than when we take our fur willingly. If your ploy is to make *her* seem she's lost her wits, you seeming to do the same should also reflect back. And remember, you must act as though the silver causes you great pain."

"And you must remain a man. I see the sunset torturing your body already. Fight the draw to change. I cannot do this alone. Not in a way that would not spill blood."

"I will do what needs be done." He sighed. "All this relies on Aldhild herself playing along. What if she just decided to take her own fur instead?"

Gerwalta swallowed, her eyes peeling away. "Then *I* will do what needs be done."

"You don't mean…"

"Andreas Baron!" she whispered with aggression. "No matter what has happened between us, I am still a *wolfsretter*. It is my duty to ensure she does not pose a danger."

"But she is a *queen!*" Andreas argued. "Her pack is too new for her to have formed a strong bond with her second. You destroy Aldhild, you leave her pack not only without command, but naturally inclined to avenge her. And on full moon!"

"What choice do I have?" Gerwalta's wide eyes flashed not anger, but fear. "I can flee an attack, but you cannot. What if she sets her pack on you? What if... I can't lose you, Andreas! I won't. I refuse to."

Gerwalta crashed into him. When her lips met his, the konigswolf felt it wash over him: love. Pure, utterly determined love. Even if Gerwalta never became his mate—and how could she, given the obvious—he would never love another. Even knowing his constitution could wash out his heart and paint it in the color of any other shewolf—he'd never allow himself to betray her.

And he would keep his laymen form, even under the pull of the full moon. For it was what she needed of him. Andreas would change the laws of god to do what Gerwalta required, or die trying.

The door of the chambers opened. They flew apart as though ricocheting off each other, creating distance where there had been none. Without hesitation, and despite having been both on the edge of tears and driven by passion just moments before, Gerwalta snapped into her assumed persona as though it were merely a scarf she need throw about her shoulders.

"Is it time, my queen?" she asked. "Shall the wolfsretter shackle me now?"

"Yes, only..." Aldhild strolled out, holding up a pair of *iron* manacles on a chain in her hand. "Use these, which you should have no difficulty in handling, Herr Baron, or I fear our little red riding hood will slip her silver bonds and go scampering back, over the river and through the woods."

His confusion stood mere moments of reflection as a man garbed in a red cloak rounded the shewolf.

"Well, if it isn't my dear cousin," Bernhard said. "And her little puppy."

# TWENTY-THREE

The glint of silver flew from Bernhard's hand too fast for Gerwalta to stop it. For one brief moment, she called out, only to find relief the next when the metallic disc warbled, losing shape, transforming moments before landing square against Andreas's hands and wrists. The sack of silver coins crashed and spilled out over the stone-cobbled floor, as did Andreas a moment later.

The konigswolf wanted to bellow; that much Gerwalta could see. But what drew her concern more were the pulsations beneath his flesh, the ripples of bone and muscles contorting, converting, his inner wolf fighting to get free.

"Andreas, stay with me!" she begged. "I need your voice."

Tortured grunts came from his throat. "The... silver..." he croaked. "Take it off!"

Gerwalta fell to her knees, working her will against the poison grafting into his skin. She reached out again with her power, willing the metal to obey. "I cannot. It's... It's..."

Her distraction left the betrayer an advantage. Bernhard swooped, slapping the iron manacles over Gerwalta's wrists, using the chain that linked the set to yank her to her feet.

"Blood-claimed silver, cousin," he said. "I believe that's the term you're searching for. The coins are as well, by the way. I knew your training would draw you to that cache."

"Blood-claimed silver?" Impossible. "That power is only to be used for the claiming of a fire medallion and in the forging of a wedding band!"

"A quaint, old tradition I've chosen to ignore, for obvious reasons."

"You cannot seriously mean that you..." Gerwalta looked off into the distance, her face contorting. "How could you run so much silver through your own heart? The pain you must have endured…"

"Will all have been worth it, once I set our world right." Bernhard yanked the chain, forcing his cousin to his side, her face to his mouth. His vicious tongue licked up her jawline, even as Gerwalta struggled to pull away. "Now, listen to every word I say, or your wolf will die."

Somehow, Andreas managed his feet, even as Aldhild took him by the arm to guide him toward the room that lay just beyond the door.

"Did you really think I wouldn't recognize a wolfsretter when she stood before me?" the shewolf asked. "Or a wolf who bears such a close resemblance to the brother who tried to kill me?"

As was the tower, so was the room: wide, round, with only one way in or out. Or so she thought, until Gerwalta looked across the space, through the flicker of candlelight, and saw another door opposite them. The tower had no external stairs she'd observed from the ground, so it must lead to the wooden parapets she'd noticed when first they'd crossed into the bailey. That could be her escape, if she could break free of her captor's hold. Only, how could she leave Andreas behind?

Begging was the desperate act of the defeated, but it was the only road left for her to tread. "Please, Bernhard. Think about this! If you expose us to the laity, every woman, man, and child wolfsretter will become their servant. We'll be exploited and persecuted. Wolves will be enslaved and sent forth as cannon fodder!"

To her dismay, her cousin only laughed. "Is not our highest calling to protect the laity from the lupine? And yet, how many laymen walk into the fields of death, while wolves stay hidden away in their forests and ravines? Our fault is not in exposing them, Gerwalta, it's in helping them keep hidden. I've done only what every Matron has been too much of a coward to do."

"What you've *done*?" As they were dragged forward, the truth dawned over Gerwalta's face. "The emperor already knows about us."

"Yes, we do."

Neither of their captors needed to speak, for in the midst of the sparse room was a single man who represented the multitude. Surrounded by six soldiers with silver swords, and with regal bearing, attire, and demeanor he fully laid claim to the title "emperor."

Though she'd had encounters with nobles, Gerwalta knew Ferdinand only from rumor and reputation. He looked every bit the caricature drawn in her head, from his oily, ebony hair which twisted at the ends, to his wiry mustache, to the armament of his prominent proboscis which ruled, in addition to half of Europe, a goodly portion of his face.

She called out as someone took a staff to the back of her legs, forcing her knees to buckle and hit the floor.

"Don't you touch her!" Andreas's gravelly voice evidenced his animal nature rearing its head. "I'll kill anyone who lays a hand on her. I'll— *Argh!*"

His cries overpowered the hiss of searing flesh. Gerwalta bucked, kicked, bit at the air. Anything to get to him. Anything to free him.

"Andreas!" she called out, wishing she had her medallion still. "Don't worry about me. Concentrate. Stay a man. Stay with me now, as a man."

"Is this the fierce warrior I was promised?" A finger hooked under Gerwalta's chin, pulling her eyes up. Ferdinand stood just inches away. "I do not see how *this* creature—this meek, crying woman, could possibly be stronger than you, Herr Faust."

Bernhard's voice came from behind her. "It is the way of my kind. The women are stronger. At least, physically. As to the gifts of the intellect, each man and woman is doled out a share as seen fit by our mighty creator."

The regent sneered as he drew back his hand and stood. A few flicks of his hand, and two guards rushed from their posts, hooked her under her arms, and pulled Gerwalta to her feet.

"And you're certain *this* is the one who you wish for your bride?" he asked. "You've brought such riches into our coffers, I'm certain a noble match could be made for you. The Duke of Saxony's third daughter, perhaps?"

"His Majesty is very kind, but I'm afraid that to take a laywoman as my wife would defeat the purpose of our agreement. If you wish for Fraulein Barvat and me to assure in a new age of lupine-led assaults against your enemies, it will be necessary for us to draw from our own in matters of family." He rounded on her at last, that vile snakeskin kin of hers, and continued. "Gerwalta is the only unwed daughter of our High Matron in the clan of Red, who will fall before me when I bring her the royal decree proclaiming my command over all wolfsretter. She, in turn, will command Gerwalta's acquiesce to me, and a wolfsretter *always* obeys the Matron. Bloodlines are quite critical for our ability to dominate lupines. I am certain *you* of all people can appreciate that."

"Yes, bloodlines are the fabric which keeps the monarchy strong." The emperor then turned to Aldhild. "Fraulein Barvat, this is the—what did you call him? I remember I found it quite amusing. Oh, yes!—the *king wolf* you've selected from your new pack? I can see he, even in his layman form, is a strapping specimen, but will you be able to woo him away from this—" Ferdinand tossed a dismissive wave Gerwalta's way, *"lady?"*

Gerwalta felt like she'd been punched in the stomach. Whatever happened, her fate had ultimately remained unchanged. Bernhard was the most likely contender for her hand when she'd left Triberg, and that would be no different if his scheme succeeded. Andreas, on the other hand... She couldn't stomach it. Couldn't accept that he'd be given to mating by force. That the konigswolf would be bonded to anyone. He deserved to be happy, to love and be loved.

Like she loved...

The wolfsretter cut off her own apostasy before it could grow roots.

Aldhild bowed her head before speaking. "He is the brother of the one I wished, your majesty, but that is little concern. In fact, Andreas is an even better prospect, and once I claim his mating bond, he will be helpless to reject me. It is imperative for the mated wolves to be dedicated to one another. He will be loyal to me and me only. He will kill if I ask him to, and for you, by proxy of my dedication to the crown. He comes from a noble lupine bloodline, one whose renown will help me to bring the other packs under my authority."

"And by mating, you mean..." Ferdinand acted out a crude gesture with his wiry hands.

How had Aldhild learned to act so demure? She even blushed. "Yes, my liege. We are ancient beasts, and ancient rites still bind us."

"Lucky bastard." A momentary, lustful curl perked in Ferdinand's expression before vanishing in a wink. "Do what needs to be done, and be cautious that the truth of these events never reaches the church. Both of you will report to me in the morning so we can start to plan our assault east. Finally, I'll have soldiers who can stand against that cursed Wallachian convert! Serve me well, and you will be rewarded handsomely."

Bernhard and Aldhild knelt as two soldiers followed the Emperor from the round room, their footfalls diminishing with every step down the circular tower stairs. At Aldhild's command, the doors were closed, and the four remaining soldiers, two of them still holding Gerwalta on her feet, remained.

"How could you do this?" Anger dipped her words in red as she faced her cousin. "To your mother? To your Matron? To your people? To me?"

"To you was the simplest part, heartstrings." Bernhard grinned, balled fists on his hips. "If I hadn't done this, your mother would have married you to me, if for no other reason than to assume my mother's Matronship once she passes. A man could never be trusted to rule a wolfsretter homestead, could he?"

"Seeing what you've done with such a little taste of power, can you find fault in such thoughts?" She leaned toward him, her voice becoming deadly soft. "Do not fret, cousin. If you try to touch me now, you'll be woman enough, when I'm done with you."

Bernhard bore his teeth, pulling back his hand, readying the strike. Gerwalta refused to flinch.

"Bernhard!" Aldhild called out. "Do not be distracted. If I do not claim Andreas tonight, our plans may come to ruin."

Forced to turn his attention, the blow remained unthrown. "I have bound him in silver for you. If he takes fur now the way I've wrapped him up, it won't be without losing a foot. He will remain a layman. What more do you require of me?"

A growl lumbered in Aldhild's chest, ripping out in frustration. "Fool! The mating of a pack leader is an auspicious event, requiring the witness of the pack on full moon. That is why everything we have orchestrated has been for this night. Either my pack must be brought here to the tower, or Andreas and I must be guided below."

"It seems that this is something for which plans should have been made before."

"If you will recall, *I* wished to have the audience with Ferdinand in the dungeons, but *he* insisted on the tower."

Bernhard crossed his arms and examined the space. "Here feels more secure than the dungeons. Though I will not savor having to witness such animalistic rituals."

Aldhild coughed a laugh. "You'll see who the animal is come your wedding night. I will return shortly. Once I claim Andreas, we will move on to the next part of the plan."

With that, the queen of the Nuremberg pack took her wolf, her fine clothing ripping into shreds, and then took her leave.

# TWENTY-FOUR

His cries had dulled, but whimpers remained.

Gerwalta wished she knew what to say, what to do. If he could take his wolf, at least Andreas could fight his way out and be safe. She *could* save herself, if only she could make it to the parapet door. The soldiers may give chase, but she'd outrun them. Only, she'd never outrun the guilt of knowing she'd left Andreas behind. Besides, how far would she get? Aldhild would order her pack to chase her down. Maybe she'd get out of the castle, perhaps even the city. But exhausted after pushing so hard for two days to make it this far, she wondered if she had the ability to go two more hours without collapsing.

"Was the plan always to take me as your bride, or was it just convenient that I came along when I did?"

Bernhard looked up from the ball of silver he bounced in hand, indifferent to her now where before he'd been so tender. "Convenient is the last word I would use. There was a moment in Ulm, when my thugs cornered you in the church, that I debated letting them kill you. Or at least, letting them try. It would have given me chance to escape without my plot being revealed. But, yes, I have known for some time that when this plan came to fruition, you were the one I wanted. Fourth daughter to a powerful Matron, trained in diplomacy and just the right age to carry my seed... In the end, I rather enjoy doing away with the artifice of formally seeking your hand through your mother."

"I could still refuse." Gerwalta put as much iron into her voice as it would hold. "It is not customary for a daughter to reject the husband her mother selects, but it is not unprecedented."

Bernhard pushed himself away from the wall he'd been leaning against and came to face her. "Refuse me, and I'll inform your mother of your..." His eyes flashed quickly to Andreas's shivering form on the ground. "...disgrace. Aldhild said she smelled you two all over each other, and I've noticed the way your eyes light up when they linger on him."

"My mother would never believe me capable of that."

Even as she said it, guilt pulled within her. How it hurt to imply Andreas was so undesirable, so loathsome.

"But she'd believe it of the wolf. Gunda was probably testing his trustworthiness as much as yours, sending you on this mission. If you survive her judgment, it would only be in exile, and Andreas would be killed, mate of the Nuremberg Queen Wolf or no. Face it, Gerwalta, you are beaten. Besides, the Red Matron has been eyeing me for some time as a proper spouse. Assured, of course, by my status as the only surviving child in a region where dominance is critical."

"And was that a convenient coincidence as well?"

Her cousin sneered. "Oh, no, heartstrings, I killed both of my sisters. This plot did not rise into existence with the dawn."

"Monster!" She pulled taut her restraints, feeling the bite of the iron manacles into her flesh. "Cur! What makes you think I would ever marry you? That I would ever love you?"

"Love?" Bernhard threw back his head and crowed. "When has love ever mattered to one of our kind? No, heartstrings, let me make this quite plain: your role as my wife will be to *grow my seed*, both in mind and in body. The wolfsretter will be remade, starting with our children. We will dominate the wolves, and be ruled as Lord God intended, by the will of men, not women. The wolves got that much right."

"But Aldhild—"

"Aldhild is an abomination!" He growled back. "An anathema, turned away by her own kind. She was on the edge of madness when I found her and found a pack to take her. She owes me her life, and I've used every bit of my influence over her to twist her to my whim. The shewolf *serves me,* just as you will *serve* me."

Her anger had heated the kettle of her eyes. Even as Gerwalta struggled to hold back the tears, Andreas's whimpers broke her. "Please, Bernhard. Let us go. Let *Andreas* go. She has a whole pack from which to choose a mate."

"Why, so he can be yours instead? You would lower yourself to be a wolf's bitch?" Bernhard spit in her face. "You're lucky I'm saving you from the folly of your feminine heart. This is why a woman should never rule."

"I would never—"

But if he heard her say that now, it would look as though she were appealing to Bernhard's philosophies. It would crush Gerwalta to have Andreas think she thought any less of him because he was a wolf.

"You would," Bernhard insisted. "His fate is really your fault, you know. Aldhild's mate was supposed to be the brother. Of all the wolves she recruited to form her pack, she desired him most, probably because he was the hardest to break. Andreas Baron was the only king to come after his lost packling. When Stephen saw his brother had debased himself, from a wolf's perspective, to accept the help of a wolfsretter, he felt the depth of his brother's love and his loyalties divided. Even after Aldhild got his eyes back to her, and I threw Andreas down the well to frame him for killing the boy, *you* had to rescue the konigswolf, didn't you?"

The events of those two days flashed in her mind's eye. It couldn't have been, could it? Gerwalta inspected the fabric of her memory like a sack that had grown a hole that refused to be found. When would Bernhard have even had the opportunity to confront Andreas? But then she recalled the way he'd insisted he needed to be the one to canvas the village, for it was the layman's world, and there a woman had no power.

The hindsight of her stupidity crushed her spirit. It was her fault, all of it. But how could she have known that by saving Andreas, she'd be dooming him at the same time?

Gerwalta drew some comfort from the sensation of the pack's approach from the tower stairs below. Now that there seemed no way to change the outcome of this horrendous series of events, she was eager to have them be done with. This battle was lost, but the war could not continue unless she lived to the next confrontation.

The doors opened at the back of the chamber, bringing with it a cacophony of snarls, growls, and clashing metal.

Bernhard turned, even as he crafted the silver blob back into a dagger. "About time, Aldhild! Take your bloody mate, then. I'm tired of minding your—Who are... Who are you? You're not Aldhild!"

Gerwalta's head shot up, seeing the balances tip despite not understanding how. Bernhard and the four laymen guards assumed a formation, squaring off against a dozen wolves, teeth bared and claws long, led not by Aldhild, but by a silver wolf with a patch of brown behind his right ear.

As the parties faced each other, all forgot about the two prisoners. She used the chaos to her advantage, falling to Andreas's side, pulling at his restraints.

"No!" He called out as she attempted to wrench the links apart. The act only drove the lip of the cuffs deeper into his wrists. "You must flee!"

"I am *not* leaving you."

"Listen to them!"

Gerwalta looked up long enough to see the guards fending against a wolf each, while her cousin had spun some of blood-claimed silver into a shield and sword, and was using it to fend off the advances of not one, but three wolves.

Andreas grasped her hand. "It's full moon, and a wolf lusts for blood. They will destroy you."

"Leaving you will destroy me, and I—"

Her words died as the flickering shadow cut across them.

The maw was more teeth then flesh, the wolf's lips pulled back so that his long, sharp, fatal fangs filled her vision. Only inches away from her face, she knew she was done for. No silver in this room would obey her command, and attacking from below she'd never be able to overpower the beast before her.

The joy in Andreas's voice sieved through the crackle of the pain. "You're alive!"

Gerwalta's head cocked to the side as the lupine settled back on its haunches and yipped. She knew this wolf. She'd faced him once before.

"Stephen?"

If the wolf's teeth weren't to kill her, his reaction might. Stephen leaned forward and pulled his tongue across her chin, the closest thing to a hug a lupine in his wolf could do. How was it possible?

And how was he rationale enough not to simply rip her to shreds at this very moment, under the light of a full moon?

"We'll have to explain the details to her later, brother." Through his suffering, the konigswolf managed to sit up. "After we've had the chance to survive. Go, do what you must."

Gerwalta wasted no time in helping Andreas to his feet. Were she a man and larger, she'd not have been able to needle under his arm and hoist him with her shoulder. "What must he do? How is he here? Who are these other lupines?"

"Later, love. We need to run. Stephen says there's a troop of imperial guards on their…"

No sooner had they taken two steps toward the door than dark-clad soldiers began to file in. A quick sweep of the room brought the count of wolves, including Stephen, to ten. The imperial fighters might outnumber the lupines two-to-one, but unless they brought silver blades or managed to remove limbs or heads, they had stepped into a battle they were destined to lose.

Stephen set himself on all fours, a barrier between wolf, wolfsretter, and the violence.

Gerwalta looked about, and caught sight of the small, wooden door on the far side of the room. "Come, this way," she said, dragging Andreas along.

"But that goes to the parapet. We'll be trapped at the top of the tower with no way to get down."

She pushed on, throwing the door open, taking in the full moon's glow like a salve. "That room is filled with moon-crazed lupines and soldiers who likely have orders to see to our retention. We'll wait until they kill each other off or move on to other grounds, and make our escape. There is still the question of what to do about Aldhild."

"We need to do nothing. For better or worse, she is dead."

"What?" She turned on the konigswolf as she lowered him down. "How do you know that?"

"Because Stephen killed her," Andreas said, unable to hide a prideful smile. "He snuck into the castle just before sunset, following our scents. He encountered Aldhild as she returned to claim her pack, and challenged her. He victoried."

So Stephen was king. Was that a good thing? Everything they'd experienced until now led her to believe not, but then again, Andreas's brother had just stood between her and danger *and* licked her face. "And now suddenly, your brother likes me instead of wanting me dead? How did that come about?"

"He does not lack intelligence, Gerwalta. He read the situation and saw that you're on our side. Also, there's the fact that you're my mate." Andreas held up his hands, wincing, blood trickling down the insides of his arms. "Can you remove these, please, love?"

She slapped down his injured paws. "What did you just say?"

"The manacles: take them off. They are silver, you know, and I am still a lupine. They *do* sting a bit."

"Not about the bloody manacles!" she shouted. "What do you mean I'm your mate? Did I pass out? Does it..." She swallowed her awkwardness. "Does *mating* not engage one's body as much as I've been led to believe? Did we *consummate* and I was not aware?"

His face screwed up. "Darling, when we *consummate,* you will be aware, in every inch of your body, intimately. *Feverishly.* But no, to the best of *my* knowledge, your maidenhead is intact." He shifted, taking her hands between his blood-streaked fingers. "You are my mate, and I yours, not because of any meeting of our bodies, but because of the joining of our hearts."

Things went from sweet to peculiar in the beat of a bird's wing, as Andreas chirped out some very wolfish sounds through his very glorious laymen face. When Gerwalta met that with only confusion, he explained.

"It's something wolves say to each other. It means, '*my heart beats in your chest.*'"

To his disappointment, she scoffed. "You're injured and you're delirious," Gerwalta declared. "No more foolishness. If we don't find a way out of here, neither of our hearts will be beating regardless in whose chest they reside."

He lifted his hands once more. "Manacles?"

Disappointment reclaimed her features. "I can do nothing, I'm sorry. Bernhard blood-claimed the silver. Only he commands it."

"Then how do we get these off?" The konigswolf shook his arm, making the chain connecting the two cuffs rattle.

"Blood-claimed or no, it is still silver. We need only find a smithy."

"Or I could remove them willingly."

They turned. Bernhard's sword dripped with blood. Lupine or laymen? Did it matter? Neither would make his blade any less sharp.

He raised a shield, though the arrogance in his face served as well, making Gerwalta want to keep a goodly distance from him.

"*If* properly motivated, that is," he continued. "Agree to my terms, Walta, and I'll let him live."

Gerwalta spun, seating herself on Andrea's lap, determined to take any blow her errant cousin may throw the konigswolf's way. "Enough. Aldhild is dead, and her pack's allegiance has been claimed by another. You have no grounds for holding on to Andreas now. Let him go."

"No grounds?" His toothy smile irked her. "So I was imagining him kissing my bride-to-be, then?"

She faltered. "He... *I* kissed *him*. You cannot hold him at fault for my—"

"Exile for a fourth daughter would be particularly cruel, wouldn't it?" Bernhard pressed on. "You do not have the combat training of your sisters, nor the ability your brother might have to succeed in the world of laymen. You'd be turned out from home, without a clan, fated by birth to be an enemy of all wolves who could then kill you without ramification."

"No!" Andreas shifted his weight beneath her, forcing Gerwalta to rise along with him. Though he still feigned when she placed herself between the two men, he did not demure in sight of Bernhard's silver. "Do not threaten me, Betrayer. I kissed her, and by God, I love her. And I will never, *never* let you or any of your kind touch her."

Gerwalta let out a hiss as her eyes closed. "Every word you speak signs your execution papers, Andreas. Please, stop. Do not hand him the very weapon he will use to strike you."

"As far as he's strayed from honor, do you think he was waiting for legal justification to kill me? I was dead the moment he knew I loved you." The width of the parapet proved just enough for Andreas to circle the wolfsretter before him. He held up his hands, displayed the bubbling, bleeding flesh warped by silver. "I ask only that you remove these chains and give me a fair chance to defend myself. I am weary from the silver, weakened from travel and turmoil. You will finish me in short order, but at least let me die as the king I am, and not the groveling inhuman creature you think I am."

Before she could interject, Bernhard grinned, saying, "So be it."

The silver fled Andreas's wrists, and within moments, where the battered man-king had stood, the lord of the lupines remained.

"Andreas!" Gerwalta lunged forward, but too late.

The wolf charged, snarling, barking, teeth-bared and dripping. Bernhard leaped, grabbing one of the timbers of the tower roof which extended off the parapet with his free hand and hoisting himself out of the striking path. The energy behind his pounce had sent the konigswolf flying, and Gerwalta cried out, fearing he'd fallen. He hadn't, but his top half hung precariously over the railing, the bottom half of the massive wolf trying to find purchase on the stones beneath his feet.

"The reason we keep to the trees, is because they so fear heights. Or didn't you know?" Bernhard dropped down, pacing. "Not all daggers are made of silver, heartstrings."

The dark, brooding look of his eye struck her deep in her gut. Bernhard was hunting, and she was the prey. Her cousin was a fearsome predator; she knew by reputation and, to some extent, observation. But every warrior had a weakness. Both cousins had been trained to listen. For a snap, for a pant, for the rustle of leaves.

They'd never been taught to listen for the silence.

Unlike the wolfsretter, Andreas learned from his mistakes. To charge? That had been a mistake. As was to attack from the front. The konigswolf moved with such determined, deliberate, delicate movements, claws retracted and maw closed, he made nary a sound.

All Gerwalta need do is keep her cousin distracted long enough…

"I would rather die than let you touch me, traitor!"

He feigned insult, splaying his hand over his chest in overly dramatic fashion. "Oh, love, such cruel words for your intended. But I remind you, I'm not the one who debased herself to tarry with a beast. Do as I say, or I *will* see you ruined! I can always find other wolves and scare them enough to do as I say. I will make good on my promise to train an army of lupines for the emperor, and I will flood his coffers with so much silver, your Gunda Faust will have no choice but to bow down before me."

*His arrogance is also a weakness. Exploit it.* "So you're saying that if I agree to be your wife, to foster your plots and serve your agenda, you will let Andreas live and allow my clan to continue to prosper?"

"Prosper may be an overstatement, but I will assure that Schloss Wolfsretter has sufficient resources and contacts to maintain its Matron. What's more, I will assure they continue to live, and that your... *indulgences* remain unknown."

With that, the man before her reached a hand to his sword, and pulled from it a generous pinch of the metal. The remaining blade immediately liquified, filling in the gap, healing. Within moments, Bernhard had wielded the small amount of silver into a hoop crowned with the emblem of a rose.

"Take this ring, and my hand, and help me lead the dark ones out of the shadows, with our kind ruling them all."

Even as Andreas tested his balance, a prelude to his strike, Gerwalta kept up the act.

She started to reach for the ring, and took it at the very moment the werewolf leaped.

# TWENTY-FIVE

Andreas had heard stories of the odd sensation one has when he realizes he's to die. As though time slows down. As though thoughts speed up. As though life comes to an end in an instant, and the totality of it stretches on forever. It had not occurred to him that saving Gerwalta would result in his death, but he could not find it in himself to be sorry for saving her life at the cost of his own. What would a worthy wolf not give for the woman he loved?

Bernhard, that cursed snake, turned only in time to catch a wolf streaming through the air, moments from contact. By the time he'd pivoted in an attempt to get his sword between them, they were both sailing over the wooden rail of the parapet.

And then, all that was left, was to fall.

Andreas settled into an expected wave of contentment, accepting the inevitable. His only regret, that he'd never heard Gerwalta say she loved him. She must, he could see the truth covered by the thinnest veiled expression, but to have heard the words from her mouth… That would have made his life truly complete.

As Bernhard's visage plummeted towards the ground, he noticed that the wolfsretter became smaller in his sight, instead of constant as he'd expect when falling with him. How odd the experiences of death.

"Didn't… you… hear me?"

It was Gerwalta's voice. Or at least, it sounded very much her, only harsher, straining, almost guttural.

It was at that moment that Andreas realized he was in tremendous, terrible pain. On his rump. A wolf's tail had not been designed by the creator with the purpose of being used as a handle, but such was their situation, for his beloved had literally caught him by it. From the pull he felt, Andreas wondered if it may actually separate from his body, leaving only a nub.

146

"Change! I... need... your hand... to pull... you up!" Gerwalta demanded, straining to tug him up to the parapet where she had somehow managed to remain.

Until he realized, she wasn't on the parapet at all.

The konigswolf pushed down every instinct in his body telling him to run, despite the fact that he was hanging in midair, held up by nothing but Gerwalta's grip, and she held up by nothing but the grace of the Lord Almighty and an ability to do the impossible.

"Change... back!"

*But if I do, where does my tail go, love? What will you be holding on the other side?*

The answer to that did not encourage him to comply in the least.

There was a choice to be made, and made very quickly. On the one paw, he could refuse to change, likely fall to his death or at the very least, to his great detriment, and in doing so, allow Gerwalta to appear to have been his downfall. It may cover their romantic tracks enough for her to return to her family with her reputation unscathed. Or, he could comply, be saved, and in turn, strive to be the death of them both.

He'd rather spend a lifetime fighting for her than a moment dying without her.

Andreas would have called it a leap of faith, but the use of any description including "leap" didn't appeal. Mustering all his strength, the wolf pulled his body in, curling his spine and bending up at the waist, even as he raged a war against the pull of the full moon above beckoning him to remain in fur. Gerwalta seemed to understand his attention; better to grab on to something frankly more grabbable on the top half of his body than to try and hold him by the... *leg*. In one consuming expenditure of her strength, she heaved him skyward, as though attempting to toss him back onto the parapet.

A brief moment of paw, and a split second of skin. Andreas reached.

"I've got you!"

Gerwalta's two hands gripped vicelike around his wrists just as the ground below tried to claim him as a victim, sending another ripple of pain as his shoulder popped out of its socket.

"Andreas!" She pulled even harder, and likely would have lifted him too, if not for the fact that, lingering in midair like a cloud, Gerwalta had no solid service against which to gain leverage. "I'm going to float us down. Don't let go."

"I thought…" *Breathe.* "…you said you…" *Whimper.* "…couldn't fly."

"I am *not* flying. I am falling very slowly."

"So you have fallen for me at last? It did take long enough."

"Keep at that, and I will slay you myself ere we reach ground."

"You will require no weapon. I am in love with you. You need only tell me that you do not feel the same, and I will fall down dead."

If he was expecting some sort of passionate embrace or at the very least, kind words, when again they stood on solid earth at a safe distance from where Bernard sat, broken and breathing fast, the konigswolf was sorely mistaken. In this case, literally. Gerwalta reached up, not for his embrace, but for his shoulder, where his arm hung at an odd angle at his side. With an upward jab, the dislocated appendage cut daggers into his sense of manhood. Like a wolf, a forest animal, Andreas knew better than to call out when could be helped. This couldn't be. At least his cry was brief and the pain equally as transient.

"Matters other than your heart require attention, Herr Baron."

"You wish to give attention to other parts of me?" He grinned, despite the truth of her words. "Your grip on my tail was amazingly firm."

The wolfsretter was rendered Janus-faced. Outwardly, she wore a scowl, but he did not believe the blush in her cheeks was from anger. Gerwalta spun on her heel, conjuring her cloak as she did. Intrigued by the development, he proceeded to follow her as she crossed ground to her errant cousin.

Bernhard did not rise, though he did lift his head to observe them. The blood would have turned the stomach of any fair maiden. Gerwalta, however, was made of tougher materials.

Andreas stated the obvious. "He landed on his own sword."

"It's silver," Gerwalta stated flatly. "It won't kill him, unfortunately."

"A fourth daughter? Who'd have thought?" The gurgle in Bernhard's voice likely meant he'd sustained internal injuries. Either that, or he'd bitten off part of his tongue when he'd landed. Possibly both. "Does Mommy know you can fly?"

"Why does everyone keep accusing me of flying?" the other wolfsretter huffed, crossing her arms over her chest. "If I could, why do you suppose I have not escaped before now?"

Andreas looked at her askance. "Why didn't you?"

Gerwalta ignored the konigswolf, leaning at her cousin's side. "Let us speak of a new agreement, Bernhard. One where you are allowed to live in exile, but live nonetheless, and you never speak a word of my betrayal to anyone."

"And, what, simply tell the Emperor that we have had a change of mind and no longer intend to serve him? Too many know for us to pull back the truth now, regardless of whether I live or you die."

"You heard Ferdinand. He's keen that the church not learn of his associations with us. There are many, many ecclesiastical ears and eyes in the court of the Holy Roman Emperor. I'm quite certain everyone who knew was in that room. Only his closest guards would have been trusted to accompany him, and they're sworn to secrecy."

"But Ferdinand knows." Bernhard's bloody smile spread wide across his face. "Or are you contemplating regicide, cousin?"

Before Gerwalta could offer her return, a blanket of growls fell over them.

Both wolf and wolfsretter turned, Bernhard for his part swiveling his head, to where a very bloody, very fearsome, very threatening pack of lupines was stalking slowly towards them.

"Andreas?"

The instinct to protect overrode extant realities. Gerwalta stepped in front of the konigswolf, arms wide, hands itching for silver.

Behind her, a rumble of low laughter emanated from Andreas's chest. "You are a darling, lambkin, but no need to fear me. No wolf in

Stephen's pack would harm me without his order, even on full moon."

"Stephen's pack?" Her arms dropped as she spun to him. "Your brother is a—"

Without letting her finish the question, the konigswolf leaned in and kissed the tip of her nose. "We're not getting the resolution to this we would have expected, are we?"

*No, in so many ways.*

Gently pushing her aside—she suspected in a show of dominance, for the sake of maintaining their audience's respect— Andreas approached the pack just as the wolf at its center, whom she recognized as Stephen, emerged. Being that they were kin, and as they all had just been through a heated, deadly confrontation with both traitors to their kind and imperial guards, she supposed she shouldn't judge them for their sentimental reunion, full of whimpering and, in Stephen's case, excessive licking. She hadn't the proper time to do it anyhow, for soon enough Gerwalta found herself observing the most peculiar thing with stark fascination.

Andreas, as a man, and Stephen, as a wolf, began to carry on a conversation.

"No, I agree, you couldn't possibly come back to the Schwartzwald now."

*Yip, yap, whine. Pointed staring while breathing heavily with ears pulled back.*

"We could seek the wolfsretter's aid with—"

*Teeth bared. Snarl.*

"Peace, brother, it was merely a thought. My suggestion, at the very least, would be to leave the Holy Roman Empire. If Ferdinand wants retribution, he'll come after you first."

*Whimper. Yip.*

"Yes, England *might* be a good idea. A bit of water between you and here would offer some security. You might even consider Scotland."

*Growl.*

"*Not* Scotland, then…"

"Gentlemen!" Gerwalta wondered if it were wise to express her frustration so openly, given a group of moon-crazed packlings restrained only by Stephen's good nature were within striking distance and she was without any weapon. "May I remind you that we are *still* in the courtyard of Ferdinand's most prized castle, having just slaughtered his most trusted guards and several of his valuable conspirators? Perhaps the pleasantries can be exchanged once we have *escaped?*"

*Bark.Yip. Cocked head.*

A grin spread over Andreas's face as he turned to look at her for the briefest moment, then returned his gaze to his brother. "Yes, as soon as she realizes it." Before Gerwalta could inquire the meaning behind that cryptic statement, he turned on her. "What of him?"

The konigswolf jerked his head in Bernhard's direction.

Gerwalta pivoted and observed with some amazement how her cousin managed to still be so smug despite laying on the ground, impaled on his own sword. "The sliver cannot kill you, Bernhard, but the bleeding will unless I take you to a physician. If I draw the sword from your body, will you swear to leave the Red Clan regions forever, and renounce this foolish pride of yours?"

"You could accompany my brother's pack to England," Andreas added. "They would be more easily settled in a new region if accompanied by a wolfsretter for balance."

"I would rather die in battle than live exiled and ashamed."

He pushed himself up slowly, even as the pain warped his features and the blood trickled down the outside of his attire. His silver sword had entered his back, on the right side of his body and angled upward such that its tip jutted out just below his rib cage. Bernhard wrapped his hands around the bloody point, bringing on a new trickle from his fingers and accompanying that which flowed from his abdomen. With a deep inhale and shaky exhale, both of which seemed to cause him great agony, the form of the sword melted, pooling liquid for a shimmering moment before it reformed, blade out and handle in hand, in the wolfsretter's grip.

"A pack animal should respect that wish." Bernhard turned his head and spit red, before dragging his tattered sleeve over the corner of his mouth. He lifted the sword. "And that's all you are, a pack animal."

Stephen took two steps forward, growling.

Andreas waved his brother back. "At ease, brother. If we kill him, even in battle, it will only work against us. Let him stay, if he wished, and sew back together his cloak of deceit. I think he'll find it more difficult without our help. Gerwalta——" He held out his hand to her. "Come, love. It's over."

The fact that her head spun hearing his endearments meant their story was anything but.

"If Stephen is to leave, take this night and the final moon to run together as brothers. I will meet you come dawn, on the Ulm road, so we can make the journey together."

The konigswolf looked at her with narrowed eyes. "And Bernhard?"

She shrugged. "He is still my kin. You raced across the land for yours. Surely I can take a few more steps for mine."

If there was one thing the wolf understood, it was family. Andreas smiled and gave her a nod. Then, for no reason she could fathom, he pulled her into his embrace, his naked flesh against her regrettably clothed figure, and kissed her to distraction.

He bit her bottom lip before pulling away. "Tomorrow, we need to speak of my intentions. They are honorable, I assure you."

A half smile ticked up on her face as she dared a looked down the planes of his stomach. "Evidence suggests otherwise."

Andreas said no more, but the look of lust that filled his eyes was enough to make the wolfsretter swoon. Two blinks later, he had shifted, and the pack made their escape.

Bernhard turned his head and spit. "You cannot truly be in love with one of them."

"Who said I was?"

"Your eyes, even if your red, rosy lips still deny it." The sword dropped down somewhat. "You know the consequences from such a union, do you not? Or was it a lie all along? His supposed errand to retrieve his brother an excuse for the two of you to get out from under the press of your mother's thumb, and under his... well, I don't suppose it would be his *thumb* he'd be pressing against you, is it?"

She ignored his barb. "How long have you been conspiring with vampires, Bernhard?"

The sudden pivot made him blink thrice in rapid succession. "What are you talking about?"

"The only lupine pack which spawns female kings is in Constantinople, and the coins in the red bag were marked with Ottoman words. I can't read it of course, but I recognize it from correspondence my mother receives from the Clan of Black." She took two steps forward, despite her lack of weapon. "Aldhild—or whatever her name truly was for I suspect that is an alias—must have come from there, along with enough trinkets to buy an audience with the Emperor himself. Silver tributes are not what a lupine would choose, though. Vampires wanting to seed dissension in enemy territory, however? If I were them, that would be my move."

"You see ripe fields where only fallow ones lie." He raised his sword again. "Will you end me or no? I grow weary."

"That's why you have the cart, and your two hired thugs, isn't it?" she continued. "Because a portion of it was promised to you if you cooperated. You *sold* your people's honor and secrets for what? Silver? Silver you did not even *earn*?"

"Spare me your lectures of honor. A leader *takes* what is desired, but force and by fury. Only a slave accepts whatever pittance his master sees worthy to give him, expecting nothing more."

The footfalls came from the corners of the courtyard. Soldiers, ones who would finally been roused and readied, pulled away from dinner and dormitories, approached with haste. Time was running out.

"Is that what you believe you are, a slave?" She pointed to the tower above. "Every man save the Messiah is a slave to something or someone. All you did was find a new master, but I don't believe it was Ferdinand. Who is it, then? Who corrupted a righteous wolfsretter?"

They fell in now, the soldiers, coming to stand in a circle about them. She did not know if the imperial men knew of her cousin, or would offer Bernhard any deference. All she knew was that they all had swords drawn, and she did not.

"You, you there!" A half-dressed man with a bushy mustache

and rosy, plump cheeks called out. *He must be the captain,* Gerwalta thought. "Drop your weapon. We have you surrounded. Let the lady go, and we shall spare you."

Bernhard spat blood. "*She* could kill every one of you before you could blink. As could I." His gaze sharpened. "You know that to be true, don't you, Walta? Even injured as I am."

"You could." There was no point in denying what was true.

"You want to know who corrupted me? To whom I am truly indentured?" Bernhard pulled back his sword, as though to strike her. "I fear you shall meet him anon, when I am gone. A monster, Wall. That's who. And I'd rather face Lucifer than him with my failure. Goodbye, cousin."

He spun, darted, swung. Mortal men were no match, but Bernhard would have them justify his own death. As ten swords simultaneously sliced into Bernhard, severing limbs, opening his stomach and letting his guts spill forth, Gerwalta took advantage of the distraction, turned, and ran as fast as she possibly could.

# TWENTY-SIX

The child who found him on the road and delivered Gerwalta's message couldn't have been more than eight. Old enough to heed direction without the intellect to ask too many questions. Young enough to repeat meaningless things like "not coming" and "go back without her" without understanding the pain such words inflicted.

Heartache weighed down his steps, Andreas's sorrows sinking into his boots. The journey back to the Schwartzwald took so much longer without her, the road harder on his feet. At least when he reached the place where fields gave way to elms and oaks, he could take to the woods instead. Five days in, the konigswolf reclaimed the natural rhythm of his kind, sleeping in the day, traversing the woodlands by night. When hungry, he did as animals would: hunt down small prey and partake of it. When he tired, he rested.

When he longed for her touch, the wolf threw back his head and bayed.

Had he read her wrong? Andreas didn't think so. Gerwalta's kiss lit fires within him, consumed him. She'd never tipped her heart fully to him, yet he felt the truth of her sentiments instinctively. He couldn't explain to any rational creature how their affections had grown, and in so short a time, but it was what it was. He *loved* her, and it had come about without a mating bond and despite their conflicting natures.

He wanted her to be his wife.

There could never be another.


The waning moon looked impaled on the edge of Schloss Wolfsretter's fortress tower, the dim light enough to illuminate the forested valley that stretched out below.

Gerwalta knew Andreas had made it back; Helga had reported that she'd learned as much when she'd returned from her patrols two nights before.

Gunda Faust grumbled. "Despite your lack of follow-through."

The youngest Faust ate the insult without objection. "My mission was only to accompany the konigswolf and to keep my eyes open at court. Making my way home with him was not a responsibility you laid at my feet."

It didn't surprise her that he'd gotten back faster than she did. No doubt Andreas gained some ground the very night they'd fled Nuremberg, running with his brother one last time before Stephen fled for England. After that, the konigswolf could have taken to four feet as soon as the forest allowed. Meanwhile, Gerwalta labored on two, using the distance and time to construct both a cover for their exploits, and to lecture her heart on what its priorities must be.

Her mother let out a guttural chuff. She did so hate cheekiness, even more so when the cheeky one was also stating the truth.

Then, seeing an opportunity to impress upon her Matron the utter disgust she would have felt doing so, added, "Besides, what cause would I have to be a travel companion to a lupine of my own free will?"

"Yes, I see how that would have been..." Gunda's unnatural youthful face screwed up. "...undesirable. But you did do as I asked, did you not?"

Gerwalta dared a direct look at Helga, all while schooling her features and her voice, desperate not to reveal her worry. "Did Herr Baron not share with you the details of the journey?"

Her eldest sister liked to adopt an air of authority, practicing for the time when she would become Matron. Or so Helga assumed she would, as the eldest righteous sibling, with the others having demonstrated no other traits which would suggest an exception to the chronological selection.

Then again, no one knew that Gerwalta could fly.

Helga crossed her leather-clad hands over her chest and clicked her tongue. "Refused to say anything more than his brother is dead, then asked me to leave him and his pack alone for a while to mourn in private."

"Stephen is dead?" Gunda raised a precarious eyebrow. "Is that

156

true?"

She swallowed her relief. Thank goodness that the story she concocted would mesh with what Andreas had said. "Yes, Stephen was killed after reaching the imperial court. But not by me."

Helga's arms dropped to her side. "By who, then?"

"By Bernhard Dreger."

Even the Matron flinched at that. "Maria's son? What cause would Bernhard have to be in Nuremberg?"

"One of his own making, I believe," Gerwalta said. The key to selling a lie was to blanket it in just enough truth to keep the deceit warm. "It was Bernhard who has been undermining our silver contracts."

"That's impossible!" Gunda protested. "I provide Maria's clan with plenty enough silver to serve our sacred duty. It would not be enough to undersell me. And even if it were, to undersell me with *my own silver!*"

Suddenly, Helga laughed, throwing back her head and cackling. "Oh, don't you see, Mother? This is just another of Gerwalta's attempts to avoid marriage. She knows you've chosen him as her intended."

Gunda was anything but amused. One slashing look cut Helga down to silence. Apparently, Gerwalta was not to have known about the arrangements. Curious, why? It wasn't as if she would have objected to Bernhard, back when she was ignorant of his scheming. It was something else, then, wasn't it?

"It will be quite impossible to marry him now," she interrupted. "Bernhard Dreger is dead."

"But you said..." Gunda pressed fingers to her temples. "Enough of this piecemeal explanation. Tell me the whole of it, Gerwalta. What happened in Nuremberg?"

"Bernhard was conspiring with a female lupine queen to reveal our kind to the emperor, and in so doing, to enlist all the dark ones in the war with the east."

She left out "under the command of the Imperial Court." Better to handle one catastrophe at a time, and only as needed.

Both her mother and her older sister blanched, but it was Helga who recovered first. "A lupine *queen?*"

"An anathema," Gerwalta confirmed. "A shewolf king. Don't worry, sister. She has also been slain."

"Good." Gunda rose from her throne. "While the number of corpses you left in your wake is more than I would have preferred, you did what needed to be done to resolve the issues before you. I will write to Maria and demand she appear at court immediately to answer for Bernhard's betrayal. But where was she getting so much silver?"

Here, Gerwalta resumed the lie, even if just by omitting the truth as she knew it. Then again, what did she really know? Nothing about what she learned in Nuremberg either indicted or absolved Maria Breger of involvement, but nothing Maria could know would be able to implicate Gerwalta's own wrongdoings. And if Maria wasn't involved, her testimony in the Matron's court would release her from any punishment.

Her mother descended the dais and raised a gloved hand to stroke her daughter's cheek. "I know you had some softness towards Bernhard. It was one of the reasons I sought to match you with him. Do not linger on his memory too long. A traitor is worthy only of disdain."

She swallowed back the lurch in her stomach. *Would she disdain me if she knew my heart?* "I shan't, Matron."

Gunda's hand dropped away. "When Maria comes, we will have our answers. You have done well, Gerwalta, inflicting your will on a king wolf in the lay world. Your father worried that keeping you from patrols would make you soft, but I assured him, you were the toughest of all my daughters."

Beside the Matron, Helga flinched for a brief moment, but she dare not speak.

Their mother continued. "You will begin patrolling the packlands with your sisters henceforth, tomorrow, after you've had a chance to rest."

"If it would please the Matron, I would start now, tonight."

Even Gunda quirked an eyebrow at that. "Zelda and Gretchen will have nearly completed their rotation now, and the sun will rise in an hour or so."

Could she sell the lie? She'd never know unless she tried. "I managed to keep the konigswolf under my control for nearly a fortnight. I do not want Andreas Baron thinking merely because we are back in the Schwarzwald, that I am any less of a threat to him."

The Matron grinned. "Very good, indeed. Go then, and bring him to heel. The nerve of him, telling *us* to keep our distance so he can mourn. What does he suppose we are, fools?"

# TWENTY-SEVEN

In the back pasture, little Jacob and Jelena Kosner crawled over a fallen tree nearly as tall off the ground as were they. Minding pups at play was not a usual task taken on by the konigswolf, but since returning from his sojourn, Andreas sought anything to distract him from his own thoughts. It also gave Wilhelm and Lisi, the pups' parents, a rare opportunity for intimacy. Perchance it would result in another Kosner pup, and blessing from the Lord if it did. The pack needed its legacy secured.

The next king would not be his child, after all.

So what if his bloodline would die out here in the Schwarzwald? Who could say if his heritage was truly so special to begin? Only the word of ancestors long dead, and an agreement among peers to consider it truth.

Jacob Kosner had come into his fur just this past summer, a strapping lad at six, and sharp as a blade. The boy's brown curls bounced on his head as he ran in circles, chasing his sister. The girl, a year younger, was lithe, but her older sibling had a keen advantage. Where a boy was one moment, a small, juvenile pup bounced about the next. Lisi Kosner would foam when she saw. Jacob's britches would be ruined— again—but such was the woe of raising a lupine child.

The wolfling nipped the little girl's ankle, making her call out.

"No fair!" Jelena stopped on the spot and pushed balled fists into her hips. "Andreas, tell him no fair. I can't take fur yet!"

He reached for the child, pulling her up to rest on his knee. "He ought to be glad about it too, ey? The moment you can, I think it's Jacob who will be on the run."

Jelena held up her two index fingers to her mouth, feigning fangs and making a yipping sound. "I will bite his butt."

Andreas threw back his head and surprised even himself with

the laugh. *Bless a child to shed light in the dark recesses of the broken heart.* He planted a kiss atop Jelena's amber crown. "Yes, you will, darling. You—"

His senses alerted almost too late. No sooner had he perceived the presence of a wolfsretter then he looked across the field and saw one standing there, out where the fences bordered the forest.

The child shook in place, but her little brother placed himself between her and the interloper, ready to do everything in his power to defend his sister.

"Jacob, take your sister back to the house. I will deal with the wolfsretter."

The little girl's voice shook. "Is she going to kill us?"

Jelena's words nearly broke his heart. The children were the most vulnerable, and the least able to understand the nuances of the dynamic the two species maintained.

"No, my pet, but that does not mean you should not run. Go now, and ready yourselves for bed. I will come to help you shortly. Fraulein Faust only wants to talk."

He hoped.

His young packlings did not wait for further encouragements; they sped off with haste, leaving Andreas to make his way across the field.

He trudged his way across the distance, all the while scanning the treeline, looking for the second flank. The Matron's children always patrolled in twos. Much to his surprise, he could detect no second party.

"You are in violation of our agreement, Fraulein Helga," Andreas called. "You are permitted to patrol around the boundaries of our farm, but you are supposed to write an official request to enter the grounds unless in cases of utter need."

The wolfsretter did not speak. Instead, her lithe hands drew to her head, whereupon she pulled down the hood of her cloak, revealing herself not to be the Matron's eldest daughter at all, but the youngest.

The konigswolf lectured his body to stay upright. "Gerwalta?"

Her words were soft, timid. "We must speak. Quickly. Are you amenable?"

Andreas nodded. She turned then, also surveying the trees for company, before motioning him to follow her into them. The konigswolf checked on his young packlings once more. In the distance, Jelena and Jacob had nearly reached the home in the center of their cleared lands. They'd be inside in a moment, and none other of his pack were close enough to observe them.

The twenty-three steps that took them away from the pasture, over the fence, and into the privacy of the trees were the heaviest he'd ever trod, weighed down by contemplation.

"Gerwalta, please. Tell me what happened. I was so fearful—"

She gave no chance to finish his query. In the time it took her to turn, Gerwalta was on him, lips to lips, mouth to mouth, and heart to heart.

Gerwalta's kiss robbed him of a man's reason, left nothing but the wolf and its hunger. Blood raced through his veins, an animal urge to quell his questions and satisfy his longing. Andreas's hands skirted down her backside, fixing a grip that allowed him leverage. He pulled her up, her legs encircling him at the hips, all as she continued to devour his kiss. Only when he took his own mouth back and used it to nip at her neck did she have a chance to speak.

"Bernhard is dead."

"Good." Then their secret was safe.

"My mother thinks Stephen is dead."

He pushed her back into a thick oak, pinning her there, using the freedom it allowed his hands to pull at the buckle securing her cloak just under her throat. "I told Helga as much."

Her hands pressed into the sides of his face. "Tell me you love me."

"You have my heart, my fealty, my..." The konigswolf threw back his head and chuckled. "Whatever you want that I have, it is yours. I surrender all to you."

Gerwalta pressed a kiss to his lips. "Do I have your will?"

"I serve you, my lamb." He pulled back her collar, revealing a tempting morsel of collarbone, which he immediately felt obliged to suckle. "I am your slave."

Her fingers threaded through his hair, pushing him harder into his labors. "Then mate."

He laughed against her flesh. "I am attempting to, dear heart."

"No, not... Not me."

The konigswolf stilled. "But I love *you*."

"Irrelevant." Gerwalta let her legs fall, reclaiming her own two feet. "Andreas, you must."

He didn't feel like kissing her all of a sudden. No, that was a lie. He very much desired it, but that same mouth which fed his heart was now saying things to break it. The space that grew between them was so much more than physical; it sank into his skin.

His voice sounded foreign to his own ears. "Knowing how I feel for you, you would have me take another as wife?"

How could she smile and cry at the same time? The wolfsretter: duplicitous even in emotions.

"I would have you be happy." She placed a gloved hand on his chest. "Is it not true that your heart will fall to whomever you first bed?"

"It's the defect of my kind, making traitors of heartstrings. But Gerwalta, how could I bed another when it is *your* body I want beneath me?"

That made her gasp a little. *Good,* he thought. *I grow weary of being the one always to burn while she can stay so cool.*

"Andreas... You must have realized this could never be. You are a wolf. I, your sworn enemy and overseer. If any of my kin learn that I've so much as kissed you, it means your death."

Was that truly her concern. "And your exile?"

Her hands caught him just below his sternum, pushing him away. "Fie, my exile! What life could I have knowing my childish desires had ended you?"

But a konigswolf in love was no easy thing to eschew. He reclaimed her hand, pulling it to his lips, kissing the back of her knuckles. "Then we'll run away."

"No! Your pack needs you, especially on the heels of losing your brother."

"They'll come with us then."

"Force them to give up their homes, their livelihoods, just to satisfy your own heart? What kind of king would force his people to do such a thing?"

The solidity of his determination turned to sand flowing through his fingers. "Perhaps if we kept to the shadows..."

"And how would I hide such a thing from my husband?"

"Husband?" Andreas blinked fiercely, as though blinded in the moment. "But Bernhard is dead."

"He is, but I believe my mother now feels this mission of ours has somehow proven my mettle. She will marry me off soon enough. Andreas..." Gerwalta crossed to him, putting a hand to the huffing wolf's cheek. "Take a mate. Give me the comfort of knowing there is someone here able to love you in my stead."

"Would that you say it once, Gerwalta. Then, maybe you could not so easily deny what your heart—" He leaned into her touch, closing his eyes, savoring the moment. "Please, Gerwalta. I would hear it from you."

"Andreas, I... I *lah*... I... I cannot."

A snap of branch, a rush of wind, and the konigswolf opened his eyes to find himself alone.

A lesser man would grieve. In fact, Andreas had been grieving since the morning after Nuremberg. But as he walked back across the field toward the farmhouse, he had to lecture himself not to skip, lest he give himself away. His wolves would want to know why his demeanor had turned about with such force and so fast. He'd have to tell his pack eventually, of course. Even the dullest lupine would notice his king take a wolfsretter as mate. First he'd have to win her hand, however. Then, he could go about changing their hearts.

Gerwalta Faust had said many things just now, but one thing she had not said was that she did not love him. Even if she had, it would be a lie. He tasted her love in their kiss. Scented her desire in the air when they embraced. Heard the spike of her pulse when he spoke of his hunger for her body. The matron's fourth daughter was just as gone on him as he was on her. They *were* mates already, in every way but the deed. He wouldn't discount Gerwalta's hesitance to submit to her own heart; he was not so blinded by his feelings to discard reality. When they succeeded in being together, their union would fly in the face of centuries of tradition.

But as he'd told Gerwalta, he sensed a change in the winds.

A new world was coming, one in which a wolfsretter and a lupine could be together.

One in which he would wed himself to a wolfsretter, and where Gerwalta Faust would be his bride.

Coming Spring 2019:

The Wolf & the Watcher – Red Hood Origins #2

The Red Hood Origins is a prequel to the contemporary fairytale-inspired urban fantasy series, The Red Hood Chronicles.

Find out more about Kendrai Meeks and her works at www.kendraimeeks.com.

Other books by Kendrai Meeks:

## THE RED HOOD CHRONICLES
**Reluctant Hood**
**Relinquished Hood**
**Ravening Hood**
**Rebellious Hood (coming soon)**

## THE CINDERELLA MATRIX
**Court of Discontent**
**City of Cinders**
**Isle of After (coming 2019)**

Please enjoy this Excerpt from Red Hood Chronicles
- Book One: Reluctant Hood...

I froze the moment I rounded the corner and took in the view
of the bar. The guy was pressed up against my inebriated
roommate like he was trying to squeeze 'Amy oil.' Apparently,
Revenge Plan B had been implemented. Mr. Too Close was
probably the hottest-looking thing within ten city blocks, but
unlike Amy, I knew he wasn't cruising for a hookup. Not the
kind Amy was after, anyways.

The barman and I exchanged a glance. I doubted he was up on
the fact that the man creeping my friend was supernatural, but
he was clearly picking up on the vibe that he was a schmuck
trying to take advantage of someone too drunk to break bread
with wisdom. I nodded to the barkeep as if to say, *thanks for
your concern, and no, there's no way I'm letting him get two
steps out of this bar with her.*

"Geri!" My leggy blonde roomie pulled her hand from the
Friday-night Fabio's cheek and waved me over with the
enthusiasm of a child seeing a horse at the county fair for the
first time. I crossed, shoving my hands in my pockets and my
sarcasm down my throat. When I got close enough, she gave
her impromptu suitor a push in my direction, only to pull him
back immediately.

"This is Donovan, and he's taking me to see some art at his
place. He'll drive me home later."

Amy winked, just in case I had suddenly become as stupid as
she was acting and didn't pick up on the implication.

"But we came here together," I said, giving Mr. Sexy-Paste-
Man the stink eye. I couldn't tell if he was on to me the way

I was to him. "Come on, I don't want to walk home alone. Not at this time of night."

Donovan rubbed a thumb over Amy's inner wrist, the vampire equivalent of swirling a glass of wine before scenting it. "Maybe Geri could join us. With your permission, of course."

His hopes were almost as high as his arching eyebrows.

Amy slapped him playfully on the chest. Dropping all pretense of "seeing art," she said, "Geri in a threesome? Bwahaha! Doubtful. Geri doesn't… Well, do anything, ever."

"Ever is a long time. Geri, wouldn't you like to try something, sometime? Perhaps even now? Perhaps, with us?"

Was he honestly suggesting I should lose my virginity in a three-way with my drunken roommate and a Mumford & Sons wannabe? This fangie must be young. Young, and not too bright. In a generous mood, I'd give him the benefit of a doubt RE: his IQ. He might be such a newbie that he'd not yet been oriented towards recognizing a hood when he saw one, or know the danger we held, even if vampire control really wasn't part of our M.O.

I reached into Amy's coat pocket and lifted the little slip of wallet that she kept her ID, student card, and a few dollars in. If somehow the vamp did get her away, I didn't want him to have access to any of her personal things. Despite his earlier suggestion, I knew Donovan didn't have a car. His skinny jeans were so tight I didn't even need him to turn his head and cough to sign off on his physical. There was no way he had space for air let alone a car key in those pockets.

I took a step back toward the bar. "Donovan, was it? Can we ahve a word?" With my other hand, I stretched my debit card to the barkeep to cover the tab before jerking my head to the left. The vamp drew Amy's hand to his lips, inhaled deeply, and placed a kiss on her knuckles, coiling her tighter in his thrall.

"This will just take a second. Don't go anywhere."

She nodded, almost frightfully, like she was worried she'd be punished if her butt slid one inch off the barstool. "I won't. I wouldn't." As Donovan turned and followed me, she leaned after him, as if pulled by gravity, almost falling off her barstool in the process.

"Can I help you?" he asked with no amount of hidden annoyance when we gained distance.

I pushed my hair from my eyes. "Yeah, you can, actually. Leave my friend alone. She's already met her asshole quota for the day."

His green eyes shimmered, reflecting the neon lights behind the bar. "I just want to show the young lady a good time, and she seems more than willing. Why don't you do like she asked and take her car home? After that, forget you two went out tonight. You won't notice she's not home until the morning."

I felt fuzz in my brain, an odd mental shake as the vamp tried his best to woo me with his power. It was no more than a brush of a stranger's sleeve against my arm. "Oh, please. You really think your mind control mumbo jumbo will work on me?"

"My…mumbo jumbo?" he repeated, going rigid. "Wait, what?"

"How old are you? A year?" I continued unabated as I browsed his features. "I've always been told your type was into Purple Labels, but you look like you hit up the sales rack at Forever 21. Aren't you Chicago clutches famous for being chic and uppity? A student bar doesn't scream out posh night club or executive lounge to me. Which makes me wonder... Is this your fang mitzvah?"

He winced when I whacked him on the shoulder with the back of my hand.

"It is, isn't it? You really planning on taking my drunk best friend as your first thrall? If she had any idea what you really were, she might be flattered."

Donovan's eyebrow quirked as his cool melted away. "You're not a slayer."

Well, at least he'd finally gotten the clue that I wasn't a huey. "Of course not. The slayers are all dead. No one's seen one since the Andrew Sisters were hot."

"But, how do you know about fang mitzvahs and clutches?"

Boy, this one's wall of secrets held up like a soggy waffle cone. One or two clandestine facts, and he was fine confirming everything I said. Vamp pickings must be slim in the big city.

"I'm a person who knows these things."

He laced his hands behind his neck, leaned in, and attempted awkwardness. Scratch that, achieved it. "Am I really that obvious? I came on too strong, didn't I? Too much cologne?"

"You could dial back a little, not that she'd be capable of picking up on your scent."

"I just thought, you know, couldn't hurt. Plus, the drugstore was running a really good special on Aqua Velvet."

"It is hard to let a deal go by. But if you don't mind, can I tell you something else?"

A hood's training in blade techniques started at age four. I could stab a supernatural before I could write my own name. I threw an arm over Donovan's shoulders while slipping Amy's wallet into a small bag I kept hanging from my left hip, clipped to a belt loop. The vamp didn't know about my weapon until he found my silver blade pressed against the soft flesh between two ribs. His eyes went wide, but luckily, his maker had taught him well enough to avoid making a scene.

"Etiquette would suggest you only drink from a willing partner, and Amy isn't sober enough to agree to a handshake."

"But I'd wipe her memory. She wouldn't…"

"You think that makes it okay? You think fang-rape is okay as long as the victim doesn't remember? Even if that were true, Donny, I would know, and I don't forget easily," I said, cutting him off and, well, actually cutting him.

Not that a nick into his flesh would do anything serious. Silver blades wouldn't kill vamps. But a knife was a knife, and making a living kebab of his kidney wouldn't exactly feel like foreplay.

"Take my suggestion and cruise somewhere else tonight. And I better not get word some baby vamp got frisky and left a body. I might not be a slayer, but trust me, my kind is just as much a fan of slicing first and asking questions later."

"And you're not going to tell me what that is, huh? Your kind."

"Human biology major. I also minor in Medieval history, but that's just gravy."

"Geri!" Amy whined when the tab got long and the hours grew short. Not the best timing, when I was trying to be all covert and stuff. "Why are you hogging him? He came on to me, not you."

An atypical Amy argument. Usually, she ranted on incessantly about how I needed a social life that extended beyond our small circle of friends and biweekly telephone calls with my dad that ended in yelling. If she hadn't just broken up with another asshole tonight and she saw me this close with a member of the opposite sex, she'd have high-fived me, shoved a condom in my back pocket, and told me to go ride that buck all the way into town. Hell, at this point, if she saw me making moon eyes at a member of the same sex, she'd probably do a back flip.

Donovan looked back over his shoulder, passing Amy a "just a second, darlin'" smile, but kept his voice directed at me. "I've been casing every bar this side of campus for hours. It's closing time, and if I come back to my maker's place empty-handed, I'm staked for sure. I have to have her. I promise, she won't remember."

"As drunk as she is, I guarantee she wouldn't. Not the point. Get out of here, Donovan. We both know your maker isn't going to stake you over one botched prowl."

"Most makers, no, but my maker ain't most makers."

"Grammar and you don't often break bread, do you?" The blade slid a few millimeters deeper, bringing his eyes and his bile back to me. "You seem to be male, so I assume you have balls. Use them. Tell your maker to get off your back and let you do your first thrall right. Now, I'm going to put my blade away, immediately after which you're going to tell Amy some excuse, then scram. Don't make me filet you; neither one of us needs that kind of attention."

He winced when I withdrew my weapon. I caught sight of a small dark red patch soaked into his shirt as he turned, but the wound would begin to heal in seconds. Donovan crossed to the bar, sending Amy into a flurry of the giddies. She stood up, and just as quickly, fell forward into Donovan's arms. He caught her, proving he might have been a vampire, but he wasn't a complete dick.

Amy's breath carried so much alcohol, even I could smell it ten steps away. She plastered herself to Donovan, playing with what could only be hypothetical chest hairs. "Now, where were we?"

Donovan's nervous smile cracked across his face. He pushed her back onto the barstool. "Sorry, babe. I just remembered I have a big exam tomorrow. I have to study."

"An exam?" Amy asked, wide-eyed. "But tomorrow is Saturday."

"Did I say exam? I mean I have a paper to write," Donovan amended. "Listen, it was great meeting you."

"What? No!" Amy practically broke down crying. She clung to Donovan's shirt, oblivious to the fact that it was ripped and blood-stained on one side. "My worst fears have come true. Geri's frigidness is contagious."

"No, really, I think you're sweet, but... Ow."

This time, my blade pierced his back. Again, only deep enough to be a warning, but he got the point. Literally.

"Maybe I'll see you again sometime."

And finally, Donovan turned to leave, all while shooting me a warning fang from behind a curled lip. Once we were alone, Amy tipped me off that she had reached the angry-drunk stage of the night by poking a finger into my chest and mustering the fury of a methed-up tick mouse. "What in the hell did you say to him? He had the look and everything!"

My eyebrow quirked, amused that my sweet, free-love, upbeat roomie thought she could sustain bitterness for more than a blink. "The look?"

"Of course, you don't know the look. No one ever gives you the look. You don't let them get so far as a smile," she prattled as I signed the slip the barman pushed across the counter and stowed my card. "You know, the look. The one that says a guy wants nothing more than to take you to the nearest bed, strip off all your clothes, and spend the rest of the night making you scream."

Maneuvering my arm around Amy's back, I spun her toward the door. Even though she was three inches taller than me, I bore her weight without any difficulty. Hoods were stronger than humans. Even without having gone through my formal rites that would awaken all my strengths and abilities, my innate gifts still made hauling a society girl's drunk ass out of a bar after last call a breeze.

 "Take away the bed and the stripping all the clothes off part, and I think you've just described the effect I have on every man lately."

"I know, and it's so Sandra Dee. My god, have you ever even kissed a boy?"

I blushed, pushing back bittersweet memories. "Yeah, a few."

She blew a raspberry, covering the side of my face in 40-proof spittle. "I mean like, a full on, I-want-you-right-here-and-right-now type of kiss. Not a peck on the cheek in the church basement." Amy was convinced every person who'd grown up in what she called the "in between places," i.e. not the East Coast and not the West Coast, spent their weekends in Bible school or shooting grizzly bears.

She continued without waiting for an answer. "Don't you ever get tired of studying all the time when you're not in class or working out? Of only ever having a social life when I force you to? Why are you always such a good girl?"

"Sex has consequences, Amy. Especially where I come from."

I felt a hitch in my breath in the shade of the memory. No, I lectured myself, moving Amy along faster. You will not go there. It was doomed from the start, and you knew it. You knew it could never work. "I'm really not that pristine; we just have different definitions of what bad behavior entails."

"Maybe, but my way is the best way." Amy fell against me as we left the back alley of the bar. The front would be safer, but after last call, it would also be lousy with police looking to make the city a quick buck, fishing out of a barrel as the bars emptied. We got six steps from the door when the world changed its spin.

I looked like a mime trying to rationalize the sudden appearance of a box around me, grabbing at empty air. Amy was gone. Just gone.